Behind *Bella*
The Amazing Stories of *Bella*
and the Lives It's Changed

Behind

bella

The Amazing Stories of *Bella* and the Lives It's Changed

Written by
Tim Drake

Ignatius Press

Cover design by Metanoia

© 2008 Ignatius Press, San Francisco

All rights reserved

ISBN 978-1-58617-278-7

Library of Congress Control Number 2008926713

Printed in Canada ♾

The publisher gratefully acknowledges
Bella Productions, LLC, who provided all
the photographs in this book except the
bottom photo on p. 74, which is provided
courtesy of the White House.

For all who find themselves alone,
and all who come alongside them

CONTENTS

"It's impossible." "It won't work." "Don't bother." This is what the first-time filmmakers behind Bella *heard from all the experts in the industry when they set out to fulfill their mission of making movies that could make a positive difference. Against all odds, somehow this little movie had a huge impact on people all over the world.* Bella's *success surprised the industry when it accomplished the following and more:*

• Bella *was the #1 top rated film in the theaters at the time of its release*

• Bella *was the #1 top rated movie of every film released in 2007 by the biggest film review site in the world, Rotten Tomatoes*

• Bella *was one of the top 10 grossing independent films of 2007*

• *As this book was being finished,* Bella *was the #7 top rated film of all time on Yahoo.com, the largest website in the world.*

• *Most importantly,* Bella *has touched and even saved the lives of countless people (fifteen lives were confirmed to have been saved at the time of this book's completion)*

People are amazed by the story behind how these first-time filmmakers made and marketed Bella *on their own against the tide of Hollywood. This book tells how they did it and the lives touched and even saved by the film.*

PREFACE

As inspirational as the motion picture *Bella* is, the stories behind the conception, making, and distribution of the film—many of them never before told—and the incredible stories of how the movie has affected those involved with its production and those who have seen the film are truly amazing.

The stories represent what can happen when individuals say yes to God. It was actor Eduardo Verástegui's yes that took him from a self-centered life to a life lived for others and ultimately led him to *Bella*. It was director Alejandro Monteverde's yes to making films with a positive message that led him to write the script for the film. It was producer Leo Severino's yes to a fledgling production company that led him from 20th Century Fox to Metanoia Films. It was financiers and producers Sean and Eustace Wolfington's yes to a script they hadn't seen that led them to finance the production and distribution of the movie. It was the yes of generous investors like Mark Follett, Fred & Ken Foote, Brad Reeves, Bob Atwell, and David Hackney that helped finance the broader release of *Bella* to the public. It was the yes of countless others along the way that ultimately led the film to be distributed and promoted and subsequently led to many of the stories told in this book.

When we say yes to God, we know not where that yes will lead or how our yes might inspire others to say yes as well. Our yes may lead to both intense joy and suffering, to positive and negative relationships along the way, and to events we cannot possibly foresee. Yet, just as Mary's yes two thousand years ago had eternal consequences, so does our yes.

God's providence is most clearly revealed in the lives that stand as a witness because of *Bella*. This book tells their story.

Bella stands as a beautiful example of what can happen when we say yes to God, and how love can transform lives. It beautifully portrays the love of a stranger for another, the love of a family, and the love of a mother for her child, even if she is unable to care for the child herself.

It is my prayer that this book will provide another avenue of access to the film, and that with the film it might serve to encourage others to say yes to God in their lives.

Tim Drake

Act I
the conception

EXT. BEACH SCENE LOOKING OUT TOWARD OCEAN. AFTERNOON

A hazy blue hue covers the entire screen. We hear the sounds of a gentle BREEZE, SEAGULLS, and WAVES washing up to shore. A patch of clouds drifts into frame, slowly making its way across the screen.

JOSÉ
My Grandmother always used to say, If you want to make God laugh, tell Him your plans.

Act I
the conception

Bella was conceived in an automobile—a beat-up 1997 white Dodge Stratus, to be precise. Mexican-born director Alejandro Monteverde called the vehicle "the white Ferrari." One of the car's doors was bent at the top left so that it wouldn't close fully. The car lacked the amenities of most modern cars.

Monteverde came up with the basic storyline for the motion picture *Bella* while driving from Austin, Texas, to Los Angeles. The long drive gave Monteverde plenty of time for thinking.

Monteverde was traveling to Los Angeles at the request of his friend, Mexican-born actor Eduardo Verástegui. Both had a desire to make films that could touch people's lives and make a difference. They never dreamed the difference that their film would eventually make.

During the trip, Monteverde came up with the idea for a story about a one-time soccer star befriending a down-on-her luck waitress who finds herself unexpectedly pregnant.

Originally, film director Monteverde had no interest in meeting actor Verástegui.

"I had gone to a wedding in Tampico," explained Monteverde. "My brother's friends grew up with Eduardo. My older brother called to tell me he was with Eduardo and that I should come to talk to him.

"Eduardo was a very successful soap opera star," said Monteverde. "He was a commercial pop artist. I had one way of seeing Eduardo, and I was doing something different. Movies and soap operas don't mix; they're like oil and water."

Verástegui and Monteverde grew up in the same state in northern Mexico. Monteverde's older brother was one of Verástegui's best friends. Monteverde's brother insisted that the two meet.

"He told me that Eduardo had changed and that he and I had a similar mission," said Monteverde. "We met at my brother's restaurant."

Eduardo Verástegui.

Alejandro Gomez Monteverde, writer and director of *Bella*. Monteverde broke the record for awards while at the University of Texas in Austin, and his first film *Bella* won the top prize at the largest film festival in the world, the Toronto International Film Festival.

The two connected immediately.

"We discovered that we had the same goals—to use our talents as a tool to have a positive impact in the world and to share a message of hope and elevate human dignity," said Monteverde. "That was the beginning of our friendship."

As their friendship continued via telephone, the two men searched for a project that they could work on together, finally settling on a boxing film.

"We wanted to make a film that would inspire people," said Monteverde. "We found one that I liked, but Eduardo said that if we wanted to make it happen I had to move from Austin to Los Angeles."

So, in April 2004, Monteverde sold off what he had, packed his belongings, and made the trip to Los Angeles. ◾

Art Imitating Life

"**T**hat's when the idea for *Bella* came to me," said Monteverde. "It's loosely based on different stories I had heard through others or that I experienced myself."

Every character in the film is inspired by an actual person, although in real life the characters never met.

"The lead character's family is my family. Like the lead character, José, I have two brothers.

One of my brothers, like Manny, owns a restaurant. A friend of mine went through something like Nina did," explained Monteverde, "but she ended up having an abortion."

The woman shared her situation with Monteverde, but he says that he was young and didn't know how to help.

"I always wondered what would have happened if I had been more mature and helped her," said Monteverde.

"I have another friend whose little sister was run over by a car and I wondered what happened to the driver," added Monteverde.

As Monteverde's mind wrestled with these questions, the story came to life. During the drive, Monteverde found himself being moved to tears. At times, he would pull off to the side of the road to jot down ideas.

"I wondered who would be the best person to help Nina?" he asked himself. "The best person to help someone who is in pain is someone else who is in pain too, because they understand each other. I wanted to create a character that didn't judge Nina or tell her what to do. I wanted love spoken through actions."

During Monteverde's two-day journey, he wove together the characters and the story. By the time Monteverde reached Los Angeles, the basics of the *Bella* script were there.

Monteverde arrived in Los Angeles about 4:00 P.M. Verástegui had an unwelcome surprise waiting for him upon his arrival.

"Eduardo waited twenty minutes and then told me that he couldn't do the boxing film we had been considering," said Monteverde. "I was confused. I had just driven two days to work with him, and yet he waited until I arrived to tell me he wasn't doing the other film."

"I told him I didn't wait all these years to give my life for something that wasn't great," said Verástegui.

At first, Monteverde thought Verástegui was crazy. Yet, the two shared a common mission, faith, dreams, and values.

By 6:00 P.M., Monteverde was pitching *Bella* to Eduardo. Eduardo's response was: "Do it." ■

7

The Actor

If the idea for *Bella* was conceived in a car, it was actor Verástegui's yes to God three years earlier that put everything in motion to make *Bella* possible.

Verástegui grew up in Xicotencati, Mexico, just south of the Texas border. He described himself as a Christmas and Easter Catholic.

"I was baptized and raised Catholic," said Verástegui. "The foundation was laid by my parents, but my faith was not the center of my life. I didn't know my faith very well, and you cannot live what you do not know."

At the age of seventeen, Verástegui moved to Mexico City to study acting. While at school and doing modeling, he was offered a position as a singer with the musical group Kario. The boy-band enjoyed tremendous success, traveling to sixteen different countries over the next three-and-a-half years.

Eduardo Verástegui, known as the "Brad Pitt of Latin America," is the lead actor and producer of *Bella*. Verástegui won Movieguide's prestigious Best Actor Award and helped *Bella* receive Movieguide's Best Picture award also.

After his stint as a musician, Verástegui returned to acting, taking roles in Mexican soap operas over the next five years. He became known as the "Brad Pitt of Mexico." All the while, his dream was to be in motion pictures.

In 2001, Verástegui was living in Miami and had recorded his first solo album. While on a plane from Miami to Los Angeles to promote his new album, he met a casting director from 20th Century Fox who was seeking a Mexican actor who could speak English. Although Verástegui's English was limited, the director encouraged him to learn some English and try out for the role in the film *Chasing Papi*—a movie about a man who is dating three women at the same time.

While rehearsing for the movie audition, Verástegui enlisted the assistance of an English language coach Jasmine O'Donnell, who also happened to be a devout Catholic. Verástegui would work with O'Donnell over the next several months.

As Verástegui describes it, he had enjoyed ten years of material success, pleasure, and everything that goes along with it. His playboy lifestyle had left him feeling empty and unhappy. He was looking for something more meaningful, but didn't know what it was or how to achieve it.

While actress, independent film maker, and English language coach Jasmine O'Donnell had worked with many actors before, she said that she knew Verástegui was exceptional from the moment she met him.

"I saw a very beautiful person on the inside," said O'Donnell.

Yet, as O'Donnell coached Verástegui lines from the film *Chasing Papi*, she became uncomfortable.

"I was feeding him lines like, 'Look at the hot women,'" said O'Donnell.

O'Donnell remembered having to teach Verástegui the word "wild," as in a "wild girl."

"It felt wrong. It felt weird," said O'Donnell. "He was getting auditions for parts that were using the same kind of vocabulary. I was teaching him words that wouldn't have come naturally to him," she said.

She wondered whether Verástegui really needed to learn some of those words, and found herself having a hard time separating the professional from the personal.

Eventually, O'Donnell was moved to ask Verástegui direct questions about the roles he was taking.

"All of his roles were Latin lovers or Latin drug dealers," said O'Donnell. "I would ask him if this is what he wanted."

She said that it was hard to be friends with Verástegui and watch him taking such roles.

"She asked me questions like, 'How are you using your talents?' 'What projects are you choosing?' and 'Are you assuming the responsibilities that you have to assume as an actor?'" explained Verástegui.

Through their conversations over the course of the next few months, she persisted in questioning Verástegui in a deeper way.

"She asked me who God was in my life, how I was using my talents, and whether I was making a difference or just using my gifts for myself," said Verástegui. "She also made me realize that my use of media impacted the way that others believed and acted. I had forgotten that whatever we do in media, we affect how people think, live, and behave."

O'Donnell recalled that Verástegui would tell her about all of the parties he was running to. Yet, as she sat with him—sometimes for hours at a time—she would see a different person.

"When I was coaching him, he seemed at peace," said O'Donnell.

At the time, O'Donnell was attending Good Shepherd Catholic Church in Beverly Hills. When Verástegui asked about a church nearby, she recommended Good Shepherd to him.

"He was trying to replace the time he would have spent partying with something else," said O'Donnell. "Rather than going to yet another party, he started working on himself."

Verástegui said that O'Donnell's example was pivotal in his own return to faith.

"She challenged me," said Verástegui. "She wasn't preaching. It was her example. She was living it.

"At the time, Leo Severino was living in Orange County and working at Fox. Alejandro Monteverde was living in Austin, Texas, and Sean and Eustace Wolfington were living in Philadelphia. I was ready to leave Hollywood," said Verástegui.

"I told Jasmine that it would be impossible for me to work the way that she was suggesting," explained Verástegui. "She said, 'Then do it yourself.'

"Because of that, I got together with Alejandro. She told me to go to Good Shepherd, where I met Leo. I also met Sean because of Jasmine. Jasmine's manager, Beverlee Dean, was also Jim Caviezel's manager, and Sean had a connection with them," said Verástegui. "She was the instrument that brought us all together."

Yet, O'Donnell refuses to take credit for what Verástegui became.

"Over time, he saw the person that I saw inside him; I just saw it first," said O'Donnell. "He's not the person that I met. It was awesome seeing him become who he was.

"I'm not responsible for his choices," admits O'Donnell. "Every choice he made along the way was a conscious choice."

"I realized that I was offending God and poisoning the culture by the projects I was choosing," said Verástegui. "It broke my heart to realize that I wasn't living for others. The reasons I was in this career were all superficial—fame, money, pleasure. I realized I had been using my talents in a selfish way."

Ultimately, unhappy with the roles he was receiving, Verástegui decided to leave his talent agency—an agency most actors would do most anything to be working with.

Verástegui believes that his reawakening was also the result of his mother's prayers.

"I was a rebel…I was called impossible," recalled Verástegui. "My mother once told my father, 'I'm afraid I'll get a call with bad news. He is lost in dangerous environments.' In response she prayed. She said, 'My prayers will touch his heart one day, even if my words cannot.'

"Here I was, in the Capital of Temptations, in the middle of Hollywood, and this lady appeared who literally changed my life," said Verástegui. ◼

"My mother once told my father, 'I'm afraid I'll get a call with bad news. He is lost in dangerous environments.' In response she prayed. She said, 'My prayers will touch his heart, even if my words cannot.'"

The Verástegui Family at their home in Mexico.

A Personal
Metanoia

In addition to the professional change, Verástegui was undergoing a profound spiritual change. The change was gradual, as Verástegui came to learn more and more about the faith of his youth.

The first step for Verástegui was reevaluating what he was doing with his career. He compared his realization to the image of a greyhound that's been trained to chase a mechanical rabbit.

"Once in a while, a fast dog actually catches the rabbit and bites it," said Verástegui. "When that happens, the dog is unable to race anymore. He realizes that he has been chasing a lie. That's how I was. I had wasted all my youth and life chasing what I thought was the truth.

"I promised God that I would never again use my talents in any project that would offend my faith, family, or Latino culture," said Verástegui. "Ever since the 1940s, Latinos have been cast as thieves, drunks, or Latin-lovers. I realized for the first time that I might not be a movie star. I thought it was the end of my life."

Verástegui turned to a friend for help. The friend was unable to help him, but recommended a Spanish-speaking priest—Legionary of Christ priest Father Juan Rivas, founder of the Los Angeles radio ministry Hombre Nuevo.

Verástegui went to meet Father Rivas.

"I told him that I realized that I was a horrible sinner and that I needed help, guidance, and books," said Verástegui. "I told him that I was a mess and that I wanted him to tell me what to do with my life now."

Father Rivas counseled Verástegui to relax and gave him a couple of books—Scott and Kimberly Hahn's *Rome Sweet Home*, and a book about giving two years of your life to Christ for discernment.

Yet, Verástegui was still struggling with God's direction in his life.

"I felt I couldn't live and work in Hollywood. I felt like I needed to disappear," said Verástegui. "I needed a humility injection."

Verástegui sold off most of his possessions and intended to go to Brazil to do missionary work.

"I was going to go there for two years to clean the dirt from my soul," said Verástegui.

"She asked me who God was in my life, how I was using my talents, and whether I was making a difference or using my talents just for myself," said Verástegui.

Verástegui told Father Rivas of his plans.

"He told me, 'You can't leave. God opened your eyes here. You need to stay. You want to go to the jungle, but Hollywood is a bigger jungle. God has plans for you,'" recalled Verástegui.

Verástegui was afraid.

"I told him I felt like I was swimming with sharks," said Verástegui. "He said, 'Then let's build a submarine. Let's do the right thing without compromising your values.'"

Verástegui felt the only way that could be done would be to open a production company. Yet, he barely knew English.

"'Even better,' Father Rivas told me, 'because then you realize that you can't do it. Only God can,'" said Verástegui. "He gave me all the wisdom I needed."

With the assistance of O'Donnell, Verástegui began attending Mass every morning at 6:30 A.M. at Good Shepherd. It was there that he first met 20th Century Fox business executive Leo Severino. ■

A New Partner

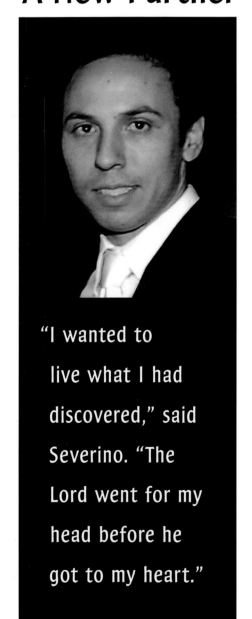

Leo Severino's conversion to faith happened as a student studying law in England.

"I thought I knew it all," said Severino. "I had no relationship with God."

In 1999, during his third year of law school, Severino discovered a small book—*The Problem of Pain* by C.S. Lewis.

"I picked that book up at 7:00 P.M. and read it in one shot, finishing it by 7:00 A.M.," recalled Severino. "Amidst a lot of tears and repenting, my whole house of cards came tumbling down."

While Severino had been hired to begin work with a large law firm, for the next nine months he read nothing but classic Catholic authors such as Hilaire Belloc, G.K. Chesterton, Frank Sheed, Archbishop Fulton Sheen, and Scott Hahn. By the time he was finished with law school, Severino was completely committed to his faith.

"I wanted to live what I had discovered," said Severino. "The Lord went for my head before he got to my heart."

Severino began doing youth ministry work, starting with a fledgling program with a dozen youth, growing it to a program that eventually included over a hundred.

During Severino's first summer after law school he

had caught the Hollywood bug while serving as an associate with 20th Century Fox. The entertainment industry greatly appealed to him.

"Everything else in law was so boring," said Severino. "At least in theater, the fruits of your labor are fun."

So Severino maintained his relationships with those at Fox. A friend of Severino's who served as executive director of the Producers Guild asked Leo if he could help establish some legal forms for the guild. Several months later, Severino was hired as the youngest employee working in business affairs at 20th Century Fox.

A committed daily Mass-goer and active with his Going Deeper youth group, Severino was concerned with how his work aligned with his Christian ethics and values.

"I prayed, 'Lord, I can't work at Fox unless you put me in a place where I can serve you,'" said Severino. "He landed me in a three-year contract in the sports programming side of things. That's as innocuous as it gets."

Severino learned the business. Several months before his contract was up, the network began merging and growing. ■

Leo Severino (producer), Eduardo Verástegui (actor, producer), Alejandro Monteverde (writer, director, producer).

Leo Severino with his wife,
Jaquie Severino, at Mass.

Holding
onto Christ

"**I** knew the Lord wanted something different and I was praying at daily Mass for guidance," said Severino, who was attending the noon Mass at Good Shepherd Catholic Church in Beverly Hills.

He can remember the first time he saw Eduardo Verástegui.

"You can't help but notice Eduardo," said Severino. "He's young and a good looking guy. You don't often see young people at daily Mass."

Severino first caught sight of Verástegui as he was leaving Good Shepherd.

"He was standing near a half life-sized statue of the Sacred Heart of Jesus that was on a pedestal," recalled Severino. "His hand was uplifted, resting on the heart of Jesus, holding on in silent prayer. That really struck me."

Unbeknownst to Severino, Verástegui was praying for guidance in his life and work.

Severino had to get back to work, so he left, but something in his heart was telling him he was supposed to talk to that man.

A few weeks later, Severino noticed Verástegui at Mass again. As soon as Mass was over, Severino intended to make his way over to meet him. He was stopped on the way by a woman who asked Severino for a restaurant recommendation.

"The lady talked for about twenty minutes," said Severino. "I was running late for work and realized that I had blown my chance."

As he left the church, he again saw Verástegui in the same place—his head bowed in prayer with his hand on the Sacred Heart of Jesus.

"I figured either this guy had incredible faith, or there was something horribly wrong with him," admitted Severino.

Still running late for work, Severino made his way to his car only to realize that he had been blocked by the same woman who had spoken to him in church.

"She backed out, forcing me to leave by another way," explained Severino.

As he was exiting the parking lot, Verástegui walked directly in front of his car.

"I rolled down the window and we started talking," said Severino. "We haven't stopped talking since."

Verástegui's accent was thick, so Severino spoke to him in Spanish.

"He asked me if I was a youth minister," said Verástegui. "I said, 'No, I'm an actor.'

"He asked, 'What are you doing here at Mass?'" said Verástegui. "I said, 'What do you mean? What are you doing here?'"

They both exchanged bits of their stories and telephone numbers.

"He told me he was working on a film, but I didn't pay much attention to it," admitted Severino. "When you're at Fox, everyone's an actor. I figured he was a bit player.

"I could tell he had no formation in the faith, but I could also tell he had incredible faith," said Severino.

When Severino got back to Fox, he looked Verástegui up and realized he was a television and film star in Mexico.

"I called to apologize, telling him I didn't know who he was," said Severino. "He said he liked that he could just be himself."

Later, Severino invited Verástegui to his Going Deeper class. When Verástegui attended the class, he was stunned by the depth of knowledge of the faith expressed by the teens.

"I asked him, 'Why don't we create a Going Deeper class in Hollywood for actors, directors, and others who are hungering and thirsting for the Lord?'" said Verástegui.

One of the first presentations was held at Beverlee Dean's home. Approximately forty Hollywood insiders attended. ■

The Birth of Metanoia Films

About a month after meeting, Verástegui asked Severino what he wanted to do with his life.

"I want to be a movie producer," responded Severino.

"That's interesting because I want to start a production company," said Verástegui.

Verástegui asked for Severino's help.

"He told me he had a staff of about fifteen people and he needed help since he would be going in a new direction," said Severino. "He wanted me to be his manager, attorney, and agent. I said okay.

"Being his manager was easy," laughed Severino. "It meant saying no to everything." Most of the projects that were coming along included negative stereo types of Latinos and were not in line with Verástegui's mission to make movies that could positively impact people's lives.

As Severino saw the projects that Verástegui was passing on, it made him realize that he, too, was being called to something more.

Through Severino, Verástegui met the Norbertine Fathers of Orange, California. There, Verástegui went on his first five-day spiritual retreat. He recalled and confessed every sin he had ever committed in his life.

"I wrote out my confession," said Verástegui. "It was like a movie script of my sins."

Verástegui spent three hours with Norbertine Father Justin.

"I told him everything," said Verástegui. "When I left the confession, I was a new man. That's when I knew I wanted to live my life completely for God."

In addition to providing spiritual guidance, Severino also brought his business savvy to the relationship. That chemistry ultimately led the three to create Metanoia Films.

"Eduardo and Alejandro had the creative side, but needed someone who knew the business and legal side," explained Severino.

Severino met Alejandro Monteverde and Eduardo at Good Shepherd, where the three attended Mass together. Afterward, they went to Verástegui's house for lunch and a meeting. There, in Verástegui's living room, the production company, Metanoia Films, was born.

The name of their company resulted from a trip Verástegui had taken to Rome with his father for Mother Teresa's beatification. Verástegui had hoped to make a film about Mother Teresa.

When Verástegui and his father got to Rome, they were astounded. There were hundreds of thousands of people there, and the closest Verástegui could get to the front was near the obelisk in St. Peter's Square. Verástegui wanted to get closer.

"I was upset," said Verástegui. "My father said it was God's will and we should stay where we were."

In the middle of Verástegui's frustration, he felt a touch upon his shoulder. A Spanish teenage girl asked him if he would take a picture of her group. She was with a group of about thirty people from Spain.

Verástegui agreed, and shared with the girl—Maria José—that he hoped one day to make a movie about the life of Mother Teresa. José told Verástegui that her mother had been very good friends with Mother Teresa and introduced Verástegui to her mother.

Verástegui shared his life story with José's mother, who said that his story reminded her of St. Francis. Verástegui didn't know much about the life of St. Francis, so the woman shared his story with him.

Eventually, the woman told how she had come to know Mother Teresa.

"She told me, 'Nineteen years ago I was drawing a picture of Mother Teresa, when she suddenly got up and left. When she returned she was holding a baby from the streets and told me she wanted me to adopt the girl,'" recalled Verástegui.

"Maria José, the girl who had tapped me on the shoulder, was the baby she had adopted," said Verástegui.

The three connected. Verástegui accompanied them to Assisi, where he learned more about St. Francis, and he also visited the Josés at their home in Spain. The artist gave Verástegui a biography of St. Francis.

When Verástegui read the book, he identified with a chapter titled "The Metanoia of St. Francis." Metanoia is a Greek term that means conversion.

"That's what I was going through," said Verástegui. "When we created the company, that's where we came up with the name."

Metanoia's first production was a Good Friday

Passion Play for their parish. They went all out with sets, sound, and three crosses. Verástegui played Simon the Cyrene. Monteverde played one of the soldiers.

From the Monday of Holy Week through the summer of 2004, the men searched for scripts. While Monteverde had sketched out *Bella*, initially he felt that perhaps they should start with another script that was closer to completion.

Severino had until November before his contract would be renewed, yet he knew that if Metanoia was going to be viable, it was something he would have to do full-time.

The three men pooled their resources.

"Alejandro was turning down a lot of jobs and Eduardo had gone two years without work," said Severino. "They were basically broke. I was the guy with money."

Verástegui had been selling the clothing he had received from *Chasing Papi*, and his paintings, to pay rent. He also had been given an Escalade to use from Cadillac as part of their celebrity vehicle program.

Pope John Paul II blesses Eduardo Verástegui and Metanoia Films' efforts to make films that positively impact the culture.

After months of turning down jobs Verástegui was a month away from not being able to afford the rent. One of Eduardo's old friends encouraged him to compromise "just a little bit to get enough money to buy a house."

Verástegui responded, "If I have to I will park the Escalade in Malibu, live out of it, and say we live in Malibu. Even though I had lost most of my money I had never had more peace in my life," explained Verástegui.

"Eduardo would say, 'It's not about what I'm not going to do; it's about what I am going to do.' He wasn't going to do vapid, empty stuff just to pay the bills," explained Severino. "We knew the Lord had a plan, and he would take care of us."

Manny Perez plays Jose's
(Verástegui's) brother
Manny in *Bella*.

When the team was unable to find another suitable project, they decided to turn to Monteverde's original idea, *Bella*. Metanoia sent Monteverde to the mountains near Lake Tahoe to complete the script for *Bella*.

Yet, money was running out. Savings that Severino figured would last eight months lasted only six. In November 2004, with only a month's savings left to pay the mortgage, at the invitation of Father Rivas, Verástegui and Severino traveled to Rome to see Pope John Paul II.

Ten days after Verástegui met Pope John Paul II, he and Severino would meet businessman and producer Sean Wolfington and his uncle Eustace Wolfington who agreed to provide the money and business know-how they needed to push full-steam ahead with *Bella*. ■

The Answer
to Prayers

Sean Wolfington, a young entrepreneur who had founded and sold two large companies by the age of thirty-five, had no previous experience in financing films. Wolfington's introduction to *Bella* came by way of a meeting between Legionary of Christ priest Father John Connor and Steve McEveety, producer of *Braveheart*, *We Were Soldiers*, and *The Passion of the Christ*.

On a Friday morning following a Legionary of Christ banquet in New York, Wolfington doubled up on his thirty minutes of morning prayer.

Sean and his wife, Ana, were headed out of the city. On their way, Sean had a strong gut instinct to turn right, even though his vehicle's navigation system was telling him to turn left. Soon after, Father Connor called to invite the Wolfingtons to meet with McEveety at his office.

When Sean entered the address into his navigation system, it turned out they were only half a block away.

"Had I taken the other turn, we would have been out of the city and nowhere near where we needed to be," said Wolfington. "It was a God-incident that tipped me off that maybe something big was at hand."

When Wolfington and McEveety met there was a connection from the start—they spent the entire day and night brainstorming ideas for the future. As a result of that meeting, Wolfington began collaborating with McEveety and was invited to Mel Gibson's Icon Productions in California.

"Steve is an incredible leader and if he is passionate about something it is hard not to get excited as well," Wolfington recalled. "He fueled the fire in me that more had to be done in media to improve the culture and give hope to the world."

While in California, in December 2004, Wolfington met Mark Rodgers, chief of staff for a

Sean Wolfington (financier and producer) and his wife Ana Wolfington (executive producer) at the Premiere at Tribeca in New York City on October 24th.

very influential Senator, who was working with organizations whose mission was to influence culture through the media. Wolfington was deeply frustrated with the impact some of the films coming out of Hollywood were having on kids and the culture.

One of Wolfington's friends not only lost his sister at Columbine, he saw his two best friends get shot and killed right next to him. It was later discovered that the boys who did it watched the film *Natural Born Killers* over a hundred times. They wrote that the film inspired the violent massacre that day—they dressed and acted just like the characters in the film.

"Ever since Columbine, I felt a need to support films that could make a positive impact rather than a negative one," said Wolfington. "Just recently my five-year-old son called his little sister an idiot. I asked him where he learned that word and he said he heard it on a TV show at his friend's house.

"The fact is that the media influences how our kids think and live and they don't even realize it," said Wolfington. "But this can be used for the good if we can make films that inspire people to do great things for the world and for others."

While Wolfington had been considering investing in efforts that could positively impact the world, it was his conversations with Rodgers that further propelled him in that direction.

Over the next three days, while still in California, Wolfington received three separate telephone calls from individuals encouraging him to meet with an actor by the name of Eduardo Verástegui.

The only difficulty was that Wolfington was expecting his wife Ana to visit over the weekend, and he planned to reserve the weekend for her.

"My first priority was Ana," said Wolfington. "The weekend was hers. I decided to leave it in her hands. Ninety-nine percent of the time when I asked her to do things like that, she would say she just wanted to have time for us, but this time, when I asked her if she wanted to meet these guys, she said yes."

Over dinner, Verástegui and Monteverde shared their stories with the Wolfingtons.

"Eduardo shared a quote from Mother Teresa: 'We are not called to be successful, we are called to be faithful.' That was what he wanted to do with his career," said Wolfington. "Right then, I knew we were supposed to do something together but I didn't know what."

At the same dinner was another gentleman who had come to seek investors for a fund that promised to invest in multiple films with a similar mission. He explained the risk inherent in making films and suggested that a fund is a smarter way to invest because it would provide more chances for getting a return through diversification in many films rather than just one film.

"Frankly, his proposal was much more logical and it made a lot of sense, but my gut told me that I was supposed to go with these guys," said Wolfington.

Verástegui hadn't yet told Wolfington about *Bella*. As they were leaving the lobby, Monteverde told him about the concept. The next day Monteverde pitched the story to them.

The story immediately resonated with the Wolfingtons.

Wolfington described his own involvement as somewhat out of character.

"I'm in real estate and technology," he said. "I never invest in high risk projects with uncertain returns. Every logical part of me said, 'Don't do it.' But I knew I had to do it."

Wolfington sought the advice of the only major producer he knew well in Hollywood, Steve McEveety. McEveety asked him a number of intelligent questions about the experience of the writer, director, cast and whether there was A-list talent and distribution already lined up. After discovering that the project involved all first timers without A-list talent or distribution, McEveety advised Wolfington to "run for the hills."

However, Wolfington told McEveety, "I agree that this sounds crazy, but I believe this is what I am supposed to do so I am not asking if I should do it, I am asking if you can help me do it."

At that moment McEveety changed his tune and reminded Wolfington that "making a movie

Eduardo Verástegui with co-actor Armando Riesco who plays his manager in the film *Bella*.

The *Bella* team flew around the world promoting the movie to leaders. Pictured from left to right: Ana Wolfington while she was pregnant with baby Bella, Eustace Wolfington, Leo Severino, Eduardo Verástegui, Alejandro Monteverde, Sean Wolfington.

The Metanoia team at a private screening where the Smithsonian Institute announced that the filmmakers would receive the prestigious Legacy Award. Pictured from left to right: Sean Wolfington, Alejandro Monteverde, Eduardo Verástegui, Leo Severino.

about Jesus in a dead language certainly did not appear to be a smart business decision but it was something that had to happen…so I will help in any way I can."

"Steve was always available to give advice and support," explained Wolfington, "and he introduced me to everyone he knew that could help us. It was amazing to have the producer of *Braveheart* and *The Passion of the Christ* as our guardian angel."

Shortly after meeting Eduardo, Leo, and Alejandro, Wolfington nicknamed them the "Three Amigos" and invested $100,000 to finance the completion of the script and the overhead to start the company. Now Metanoia had four partners and later added a fifth when Wolfington got his uncle, Eustace Wolfington, involved.

"I knew I wanted to get involved, so I called my uncle Eustace to see if he had an interest as well," explained Wolfington. "Eustace is an incredibly wise man and one of my best friends so I try to get him involved in everything I do."

Eustace Wolfington is the visionary businessman who invented the modern day automotive lease, the husband of Marcy Wolfington, and a proud father of ten children. Like his nephew Sean, he had never before invested in a motion picture but was drawn in from the beginning.

"Sean had met the Metanoia team in Los Angeles," recalled the elder Wolfington. "In December, Sean brought the team to my office in King of Prussia, Pennsylvania. They hadn't even finished their script, but they made their pitch. Before the night was over something inside me told me to take a shot with these guys. There was an immediate sense of trust."

"I have never seen my uncle make a business decision like this so quickly. It was a confirmation for me that something bigger was involved," explained Sean Wolfington.

Although neither Sean nor Eustace was familiar with investing in high-risk films, and there was no finished script at that time, both agreed to back the film financially. As time passed, Eustace proved to be a wise adviser at every level and Sean felt called to do more than mere monetary investment.

As he was discerning what role he was supposed to play with Metanoia beyond being an investor and partner, Sean Wolfington felt moved to help run the company. At this time, however, he was running another company he owned, BZ Productions, a high growth technology company that was experiencing 3,000-percent annual growth.

While at a Christian Leadership Conference, Wolfington had heard Bill Hybels from Willow Creek Church give a talk about "the second calling," and about how the Apostle Paul had been obedient to God's plan to his death.

"The talk explained how Paul was called away from the new church he founded to go to Jerusalem," said Wolfington. "Despite the fact that his new church was bearing incredible fruit,

Paul was obedient and went to Jerusalem against the advice of a prophet who told him he would spend the rest of his life in jail if he went. In response to the prophet's warnings, Paul proclaimed that he would gladly die for Christ, and did in fact do so in Jerusalem. After hearing Paul's conviction the prophet agreed and encouraged his God-given mission.

"After hearing this story I realized that I was being called in a new direction and that I had to be willing to die financially and professionally if need be," said Wolfington.

"It was interesting because the closest person to a prophet in the film industry that I knew, Steve McEveety, told me to not make such a risky investment, but after hearing my conviction he encouraged me just like the prophet did in Paul's journey."

Months later Wolfington received an incredible offer to buy his company and sold it before *Bella* was shot. "As a result I could focus full-time on *Bella*," explained Wolfington.

"At the time I was still uncertain why God wanted me, someone with no experience at all, to pursue this mission," said Wolfington.

McEveety then introduced Wolfington to Michael Flaherty, founder and president of Walden Media, the makers of *Narnia, Charlotte's Web, Amazing Grace*, and many other great films.

At dinner Wolfington told Flaherty what he was thinking about when Flaherty responded,

Alejandro Monteverde (center) with his good friend and cinematographer Andrew Cadelago (right) and assistant director Glen Trotiner (left).

"Five years ago I was running charter schools. Now I'm making *The Chronicles of Narnia*. What other reason could there be but God?"

"It hit me like a Mack truck," said Wolfington. "I realized that I didn't have experience, but neither did Jesus' disciples—this company will succeed through his strength not our own. After that moment I dove in head first and we had a group of advisers that any new company could only dream of—Steve [McEveety], Mark [Rogers], and Mike [Flaherty] helped us more than we could have ever imagined."

One of the first people Flaherty introduced to the *Bella* team was John Logigian, a co-founder of Walden Media and industry veteran. "We needed a lawyer who knew the entire industry and had experience running a production company, and we happened to find the best guy in the industry through Mike," said Wolfington. "He helped Leo write all our important business contacts and was a key advisor to us throughout the entire process. This was a team that only God could assemble in the short period of time we had—it was a foretaste of the many miracles to come." ■

Act II
birth pangs

FROM THE SCRIPT...

EXT. HACIENDA SANCHO PANZA
PATIO DINING AREA. AFTERNOON

Nina and José sit across from one another. A waiter, JOHANNES, waits for their order.

JOSÉ

You like paella?

NINA

Yeah.

JOSÉ

Alright, we'll have your Mejillones and paella for two.

JOHANNES

Okay.

Johannes leaves.

JOSÉ

Paella is full of the things you need for a child.

NINA

Who said I was having a child?

JOSÉ

You did.

NINA

No, I said I was pregnant.

Johannes comes with drinks and places them on the table.

Act II

birth pangs

With financial backing, the *Bella* team could now proceed with the film's production. There were many hurdles to clear, however, before filming could begin, and no guarantees that the finished product would ever end up in theaters. There were the difficulties of locating a lead actress, filming in New York City on an extremely limited budget, securing a distributor, and promoting the film.

The story of the film's production, distribution, and promotion is the story of a series of individuals who said yes to *Bella*, sometimes working for months with little or no pay.

Among the first to say yes was Anna Villareal, a former UCLA pre-med student who had come to know Severino through his youth ministry program.

Villareal started helping Metanoia, but eventually realized she couldn't do both pre-med and Metanoia full-time. As a result, Villareal quit her pre-med program to handle logistics full-time for Metanoia. She was the first of many involved with the film to take a path that made little sense to the outside world.

A Leap
of Faith

"**E**ach person involved believed that this was a special film and took a leap of faith," said Wolfington. "The lead actor, the director, the lead actress, and the line producer all had other projects they could have done, but they all felt they were supposed to do this film."

Since the film was their first movie project, one big hurdle the *Bella* team had to overcome was finding an experienced line producer to develop a budget and a schedule for shooting. "The line producer is one of the most important jobs on the set and we needed a very experienced person to help make up for our lack of experience," said Wolfington.

"Everyone was telling us it was impossible to shoot a $3 million film in New York City and stay on budget," said Wolfington. "They said it was impossible because it's so uncontrollable, but Alejandro insisted that *Bella* be shot in New York, and he was right."

Wolfington turned to experienced producer McEveety for assistance.

"Steve reached out to a friend to find a list of people in New York," said Wolfington. "He gave us a list of fourteen people. We contacted them and met with one—Denise Pinckley. Once we met with her it was over. She was an experienced all-star.

"Finding her was a miracle for us," admitted Wolfington. "She passed on an $80 million film to do *Bella*. At the time she said she didn't know why she was doing it, but she realized that she wanted to be part of something meaningful and positive. She was attracted to the beauty of the story and to Alejandro's vision."

Pinckley played a key part in the team's ability to shoot the film in twenty-four days and stay within budget in New York City. She worked with Alejandro to negotiate great deals with the unions and key personnel to help the team make it happen.

In the end, the *Bella* team gave Pinckley a producer credit for her work on the film. "Denise helped with every part of the production and *Bella* would not have been the same without her," acknowledges Monteverde. ■

The Leading
Lady

Another difficulty facing Metanoia was finding the right leading lady to play opposite Verástegui. Actress Tammy Blanchard was the first person to audition for the part, but originally Monteverde wasn't sure she was right for the role of Nina.

Blanchard said that she was moved by *Bella*'s script.

"I remember after reading it, I closed the script and cried for about twenty minutes," said Blanchard. "Life is so hard. There are so many people who don't have friends or family. Here was a girl who saw the need in someone else. The film offered this sense of hope."

Monteverde auditioned several other actresses, but Blanchard didn't give up. She wrote the director a letter that said, "You can look far and wide, but I'm Nina. That part is for me and I'm her."

"I told him, 'I know this girl. I grew up with someone like this who was broke and alone and if she had been pregnant wouldn't have known what to do,'" said Blanchard. Blanchard's own mother raised her children on her own, as did Blanchard's Aunt Kathy.

"I based my conception of Nina around my Aunt Kathy," said Blanchard. "I would walk with her and hear her talk about how hard it was for her to raise a child alone. I memorized her walk and played out all the emotions that she told me about."

In the end, Monteverde was moved by Blanchard's passion and persistence.

> "I remember after reading it, I closed the script and cried for about twenty minutes," said Blanchard.

Tammy Blanchard, the lead actress who plays Nina, is an Emmy award winning actress who delivered another award winning performance in *Bella*.

"I watched the made-for-TV movie *Judy Garland* which Tammy starred in and I could see that she created characters," said Monteverde. "I told her I would give her the part."

Only one obstacle stood in Blanchard's way.

She was set to begin filming for *The Good Shepherd* with Matt Damon, Angelina Jolie, and Robert DeNiro at about the same time and was worried that scheduling conflicts would prevent her from doing *Bella*. She told Monteverde that if the conflict couldn't be worked out, she would choose *Bella*.

At first the producers of *The Good Shepherd* weren't sure it could work. Ultimately, they worked with Blanchard's schedule, allowing her to do both films.

"Tammy is an amazing actress and person—*Bella* would not have worked without her," said Monteverde.

"Tammy was so easy to work with because she is incredibly talented. She is remarkable," said Verástegui. ◼

"We saw our part as interceding and praying for them," said Father Fletcher. "They would return after a long day of shooting and we would ask them how it went. It led to a beautiful relationship."

Tony Hayden, a friend of the Wolfingtons, introduced the team to the Franciscan Friars of the Renewal in the Bronx before the film was shot. The Friars adopted the *Bella* team and invited Verástegui and Severino to live at their monastery during filming. Here the Franciscans are gathered at a movie theater with Jason Jones, an executive producer, who was on the ground in New York City to help promote *Bella* on the streets.

Friars and Filmmakers

As the filmmakers were getting ready to shoot in New York City, they wanted to prepare with a religious retreat. They turned to the Bronx-based Franciscan Friars of the Renewal.

"Five days before they started filming, they came," said Father Luke Fletcher, director of vocations for the community. "We gave them a little retreat."

The friars and the filmmakers hit it off well. In the end, the friars invited the filmmakers and actors to stay at their friary in Harlem during the film's shooting.

Between mid-August and mid-September of 2005, Severino, Verástegui, and some of the other crew and actors stayed with the friars.

"We saw our part as praying for them," said Father Fletcher. "They would return after a long day of shooting and we would ask them how it went. It led to a beautiful relationship."

It also led to something more.

The friars put the word out to other religious communities, getting them to pray for the project. Fletcher said that it was common to find Verástegui and others praying at all hours of the night in the friary chapel. Severino said that several nights Verástegui fell asleep in the chapel.

The friendship that developed led the filmmakers to invite Father Fletcher and Brother Paschal Coby to appear as non-union extras in the film during a subway scene.

Father Fletcher said he witnessed what he described as miracles during the filming.

"They were on location, filming on a low budget outdoors in New York. If they had a few days of rain it would have killed the film," said Father Fletcher. "On one of the last days they needed some outdoor footage and it was raining. Alejandro went against everyone's good judgment and decided to film anyway."

According to Father Fletcher, it was raining all over New York, but in the three-block radius where the filmmakers were shooting there was no rain.

"We were back at the friary praying," said Father Fletcher. "Even the secular people were saying it was weird. They described that as a miraculous day."

Smaller "miracles" took place during the filming as well.

"A lot of things happened that normally wouldn't happen," said Eustace Wolfington. "Members of the cast and set returned to their faith. Many good things happened."

Sean Wolfington recalled a moment on the set when tensions were running high.

"It was chaotic," said Wolfington. "At one point it appeared that there was a lack of chemistry. A lot of people thought Eduardo wasn't hitting the role—especially Eduardo himself—and if either he or Tammy weren't hitting the role, the film was dead."

Eduardo shared his fears with Wolfington.

"I don't mind if this is my final role, if I have to crucify my career," he told Wolfington. "But I can't take down your money and Leo and Alejandro's career with me. I can't do that."

"Eduardo's eyes filled with tears and I saw how hard it was for him to imagine that he might hurt us," said Wolfington. Moments later, Wolfington recalled looking across the set and seeing Eduardo huddled down talking with a catering girl.

"I knew what he was doing," said Wolfington. "I could tell he was sharing the love of Christ with this girl, and a deep peace came over me like a warm breeze. I knew that if that girl was changed forever, it was worth all the money. It isn't our money anyway; we are only stewards of the resources entrusted to us. I thanked God that I was working with guys who loved him and were serving him.

"When I saw Eduardo's suffering on the set, I could see he thought he was taking our careers down with him. He was 'bleeding' on the set," said Wolfington. "But he didn't give into the fear; instead, it led him to spend more time on his knees."

After that moment on the set, Verástegui seemed to lose himself in the part. He offered up the misery and frustration that he was experiencing, focusing entirely on the role and serving others. By doing so, he was able to hit the role perfectly.

"Those twenty-four days of shooting were like being on the cross," said Verástegui. "I abandoned myself and cried, 'Lord, you're in control. My desire is to do something for you and others."

Ironically, in the film's first test screening before a large focus group, Verástegui received the highest scores of anyone in the movie. ■

Their Faith Is What Fuels Them

The one common denominator among the *Bella* team is that all of them have had a profound change in their lives, a metanoia. These changes have led them to where they want to make movies that celebrate the good, the true, and the beautiful.

"My faith is the center of my life, and I want to use my talents to make movies that honor God and celebrate the beauty of faith, family, and life," explained Verástegui.

"Our faith guides and fuels everything we do. This does not mean that we want to make religious movies, but we do want to make movies that not only entertain but also inspire people to love more, forgive quicker, appreciate life, give more, complain less, and build a better world," said Wolfington.

"We believe that everyone has been created to fulfill a mission," added Wolfington. "Our hope is that our films will inspire people to find and fulfill their God-given purpose while they are here on earth for this short period of time."

"From earliest times, the Church has been the

"It was amazing to see the transformation of all those involved in the movie, ...their growth spiritually and as a team in the midst of all the difficulties," said Father Connor. "They were an amazing example of keeping Christ at the center of their mission."

Father John Connor, founder of the Lumen Leadership Institute, introduced Sean Wolfington to Steve McEveety which led to Wolfington meeting Verástegui, Monteverde, and Severino. Fr. Connor also provided spiritual direction and support to the Metanoia team during the filming and release of *Bella*.

Leo Severino (left) and Eduardo Verástegui (right) at one of the many prayer pilgrimages the filmmakers took during the making of *Bella*.

source of incredible music and art," noted Severino. "Musicians and artists such as Fortunatus, Giotto, Palestrina, and Michelangelo created inspired works that reveal the beauty and the wonder of the world God created. We at Metanoia want to do the same today. There is a new generation of filmmakers who want to live out their faith in art and in everything they do just as Christians throughout the ages have done."

The Metanoia team is made up of a group of zealous young Catholics who take their faith very seriously and who genuinely want to live it out in their company and in the making of their films.

Legionary of Christ priest Father John Connor got involved with the film through his connection with Sean Wolfington. The two had first met in 2000. Father Connor later introduced Wolfington to Steve McEveety, producer of Mel Gibson's *The Passion of the Christ*, and Wolfington ended up doing work for Icon Productions helping to market *The Passion*. After Metanoia Films was created, Wolfington asked Father Connor to give the team spiritual direction.

During the filming of *Bella*, Father Connor helped arrange to have Mass celebrated on the set every day. Most of the time it was at 6:00 A.M.; other times it was celebrated in the afternoon or evening after filming was completed.

Father Connor also arranged a retreat for Metanoia on August 15, exactly one year after the beginning of the film's shooting in New York. The retreat was held at the Legionaries of Christ seminary at Thornwood with an emphasis on charity and unity.

"It was amazing to see the transformation of all those involved in the movie, to see their growth spiritually and as a team especially in the midst of all the difficulties," said Father Connor. "They were an amazing example of keeping Christ at the center of their mission."

Verástegui's faith was evident to many people throughout the film's production and marketing.

Corby Pons, one of the people on the grass-roots marketing team, told the story of getting into a cab with Eduardo during a screening trip to Cleveland, Ohio.

"The cab driver began talking about her relationship with her husband. She had had a rough childhood and didn't believe in a God," recalled Pons. "Eduardo listened to every word during the thirty to forty minute ride. By the time we reached our destination, she was in tears, profusely thanking Eduardo for listening, for his words of wisdom, and for lovingly sharing his faith with her."

At screenings, Pons said that Verástegui would often sit in a separate room praying not for the success of the film, but that each of the individuals watching it would come to know Christ.

Pons would chide Verástegui.

Eduardo serving children through his foundation dedicated to helping those who are less fortunate.

"You'd better be praying for the film's success, Eduardo. Pray for it, for the love of God," Pons would say.

"Eduardo's response was: 'No, brother, let's pray for the people. The film is just a means to reach the people.'

"All these people—volunteers, influencers—that Eduardo, Leo, Alejandro, and Sean spent time with . . . When we released the film theatrically, people had been so inspired by them that they went to bat for us."

As one example, Pons recalled a couple in Houston who were so inspired that they bought all the seats in two theaters when the film opened. "As an Evangelical Christian I had never met Catholics like these guys. They are so in love with Christ and devout in their faith, and they are eager to share their love with others. It was very impressive," added Pons.

Pons also told the story of a memorable plane ride he shared with Eduardo from El Paso to Orlando.

"We had a tour of three cities. Eduardo had been on the road for three weeks. He was living out of his suitcase and was so exhausted," said Pons.

When they got on the airplane, it was very crowded and Verástegui was bumped up to first class.

Pons text-messaged Verástegui: "You lucky dog! That's a big cross you have up there on your back."

The next thing Pons knew, Verástegui had come back and told Pons that he had talked to the stewardess and got him a seat in first class, up in Row 3.

"I got up there and it was the most natural feeling in life," said Pons. "All of a sudden the plane starts moving, but Eduardo hasn't come back. I look back and there's Eduardo sitting in the very last row of the plane, in my seat, next to two of the biggest dudes.

"I texted him saying, 'Eduardo, what are you doing?'

"He wrote me, 'Enjoy, brother. We are called to serve each other,'" said Pons. "He did things like that—serving people, listening to them, praying with them, and buying them a meal—in every city."

The common faith of the entire team was key during times of doubt.

"One thing we all have in common is that we're all desperately depending on God despite our individual weaknesses," said Wolfington. "With his help we can do what he wants us to do.

"We are so grateful that God cares enough about us that he included us in this wonderful mission," said Wolfington. "It has been an unbelievable blessing."

The team often spoke about the fact that hundreds of people came out of nowhere selflessly to support *Bella* and its mission. "So many people felt called to volunteer to help our little film, and that is why it has had such a big impact," said Wolfington.

"The Lord sometimes asks us to do crazy things for him," added Wolfington. "A lot of people said yes to him, and their yes inspired others to say yes.

"People often say that it's difficult to follow God's will, but his plan has always worked out a lot better than any plan I have ever come up with," concluded Wolfington. "We have all done our best to say yes to God and it has been an incredible and meaningful adventure that we could never have imagined on our own."

In the end, the filmmakers shot as many as eight script pages per day—far more than average—and ended up completing the shooting within budget. The team spent the fall of 2005 editing the film. ■

bella
The Big Win in Toronto

Once the initial editing was done, the Metanoia team tried to get the movie distributed. "We knew that film festivals were where the distributors were, and they are the best place to promote a movie since all the press attends also," said Severino. "So we looked at the biggest and best festivals coming up and discovered the Toronto International Film Festival. We rushed to see if we could get a rough cut into the festival."

Metanoia sent their first completed print of *Bella* to the Toronto International Film Festival in February of 2006.

"It was a big risk," said Severino. "We hadn't tested it or screened it for anyone. It had music, but not the music that's in the film now. We sent it on a wing and a prayer."

Four months later, in June, Severino received a telephone call from the co-director of the Toronto festival.

"It was a crazy call—very atypical," said Severino. "She told us she loved the film, was moved by it, and wanted to put it in the festival. She explained that a little more than three hundred films are accepted out of over six thousand submitted, so it might be hard to convince the selection team to pick *Bella*.

"Since she loved the film so much, she had recruited a dozen diverse people to view the film privately for their reaction. She instructed them not to talk about it with anyone, but simply to email her with their opinion of the film.

"Ten of the twelve absolutely loved it. Two of the twelve thought it was good. No one felt bad about it. She then took that information to the festival director and got the film into the festival.

"She also chose the film as one of her top ten picks and wrote a column," said Severino.

According to Severino, season ticket holders go to see the films on that list. As a result, when

Bella opened at the Toronto Film Festival, not only were the theaters sold out, but there were lines for the film going out the doors.

The entire Metanoia team attended the festival, which was held September 7–16, 2006.

"We felt like very little fish swimming in a huge pond," said Severino.

To improve their chances, the *Bella* team recruited a team of over twenty volunteers to promote the movie around the festival by handing out guides highlighting *Bella*.

All the major distributors from around the world attend Toronto, and *Bella* had a good chance of finding a distributor there while getting great publicity for its release. *Bella*'s agency advised them to have a party after the world premiere so distributors could attend. They said there was a good chance for a bidding war if they liked the movie.

"So we set up a nice party at our hotel, we all dressed up, and went to the world premiere screening with more than six hundred people who bought tickets. It was amazing!" explained Wolfington.

"The crowd loved the movie and they applauded for minutes—we were really excited," said Severino. "We ran to the party to ask our agency to introduce us to the different distributors, but we quickly learned that none showed up at the party." Supposedly there was another big film that night and the few that came to the *Bella* screening left early within the first twenty minutes."

Wolfington confessed, "We were like a group of teenagers all dressed up for the prom but our dates did not show up. At that moment clouds of doubt rolled over us because our big chance was gone. As I was walking to the bathroom with my head slumped down, I noticed that a large part of the *Bella* team was in the hallway slumping their heads as well.

"I asked God what was going on. Suddenly I was reminded of Jesus coming to the aid of Peter on the shore at the last minute to save the day. After fishing all night in the best of conditions, Peter and his team of expert fisherman came up empty handed, much like us. After all their efforts had been exhausted, Jesus arrived and asked them to throw out their nets one more time,

Alejandro Monteverde accepts the People's Choice Award for *Bella* and says, "I hope I don't wake up and discover I was dreaming." The People's Choice Award is the top prize at the Toronto International Film Festival. Previous winners include Oscar award winning films *Chariots of Fire*; *Life is Beautiful*; *American Beauty*; *Crouching Tiger, Hidden Dragon*; and *Hotel Rwanda*; among others.

during the day, into the shallow water—the worst conditions for fishing. With nothing more than their faith they threw out their nets and with the help of Christ their nets were full!

"At that moment I realized that this is how he [Christ] works: he does not deliver the fish right away—at least not in my life. He typically appears in the very last moment, giving us an opportunity to trust. So I ran over to the team and told them what I just realized and my clouds were replaced with a ray of hope," explained Wolfington.

A few days went by and still no distributors showed any interest in *Bella*. Ryan Wolfington, Sean's twin brother, reflected on this difficult time in *Bella*'s history.

"Things were not looking good for finding a distributor, but the team still had a small flame of hope flickering in their hearts. I remember Sean coming over to the group and saying, 'I think it's great that we haven't found a distributor—that must mean we need to do it ourselves.' Then he said that Eustace and he would continue to finance the promotion and distribution of *Bella*."

By this time most of the big producers and studios had left because they usually only attend the busier first half of the festival. For some reason the *Bella* team stayed the entire ten days until the very last minute when one of many miracles took place.

No one expected *Bella* to win anything, but they did not realize who was behind the movie. "While the other films had the biggest studios in the industry behind them, we had the Holy Spirit," said Severino.

In Toronto, while it was the film *Death of a President* that garnered all the headlines along with blockbusters like *Departed, All the King's Men, Babel, Bobby*, and many others, *Bella* took the filmmakers and festival organizers by complete surprise when it won the coveted People's Choice Award, the top prize at Toronto.

The entire team was in shock as tears spontaneously flowed down their faces. "We knew he [Christ] would show up to save the day. That's what meant the most—it was beautiful to see him at the shore," said Wolfington.

While Monteverde had produced films and won many awards in film school, this was his first award for a full length motion picture.

"I really hope that this is not a dream and that I don't wake up at film school," said Monteverde afterwards. "This festival is my first festival, it's my first film. It's my first everything."

With the People's Choice Award under their belts, the filmmakers hoped that a distributor would be soon in coming. When that didn't happen, they continued with their plan to finance the distribution themselves. ■

Bella Could Not Find a Distributor

Metanoia had one of the best agencies in the business working hard to find a distributor for *Bella*. Yet, they couldn't seem to find a distributor.

"We were told that we should get a distributor quickly after winning the Toronto International Film Festival," said Monteverde.

Taking top prize at Toronto was a meaningful accomplishment because it is the biggest festival in the world and many previous winners went on to win the Oscar for best picture including *Chariots of Fire*; *Life Is Beautiful*; *Hotel Rwanda*; *Crouching Tiger, Hidden Dragon*; and many others.

"Unfortunately all the distributors passed and we were left with a big decision—to invest more time and money or to take our losses and put *Bella* in our private library for our family and friends to see," said Wolfington.

"Every distributor said pretty much the same thing—that *Bella* did not have enough edge," added Wolfington. When the filmmakers asked what an "edge" was, they learned that it meant it did not have enough drugs, sex, and violence.

While distributors were passing on the movie, audiences were begging the *Bella* team to bring the film to their local theater. Because of the belief and support of the people, the team was inspired to distribute the movie on their own despite the doubts of the industry. So convinced were they of *Bella*'s worth that the team agreed to set aside their careers to go around the country promoting the film to leaders and organizations, and the Wolfingtons financed the strategy.

"Our goal was to ask people to pre-purchase enough show times so we could guarantee the successful release of *Bella*. After over a year of promoting *Bella*, close to five hundred people volunteered to buy out an entire screening of the film on opening weekend. People pre-purchased enough screenings to ensure *Bella* had a successful opening weekend before the film even opened," explained Wolfington. ■

Building Coalitions

Even when they rented a distributor's system to release their film, it became obvious that Metanoia wouldn't have a large promotion and advertising (P & A) budget like most big studio films. Therefore, Metanoia realized they would need an alternative way of marketing to build an audience for the film.

The *Bella* team built a grass-tops marketing strategy that targeted the leaders in the top fifty markets. Grass-tops marketing is building coalitions with the leaders of like-minded organizations.

"We wanted to get a message of love, grace, and humility to the Ninas of the world."

"Our goal was to recruit the support of grass-tops leaders to promote and pre-purchase entire showings in theaters for *Bella* in each market," Wolfington explained. "We screened the film for grass-tops leaders and asked them to volunteer for one of many actions that were on a survey they received after the screening."

After designing the strategy, Metanoia recruited a team of paid and volunteer people to help implement different parts of the strategy. Erin McCrory, Jeff Hunt, Corby Pons, and Ted Royer were among the initial team members that helped implement the plan.

A lot of people worked together to make the strategy work. The Three Amigos and Wolfington had already traveled the country to connect with the leaders of the largest organizations while the support team began to follow up with all the contacts that were made. Corby Pons followed up with Hispanic, Christian, and adoption leaders as a part of the grass-tops campaign while Hunt handled the film's grass-roots outreach. Ted Royer led the efforts for publicity, and Erin McCrory focused on Catholic outreach.

Corby Pons, a legislative aide to North Carolina Congressman Walter Jones, first met Verástegui and Wolfington in December 2006 while volunteering with his wife at an event in New York.

"My wife always tells me I'm the best looking guy in the room," said Pons, "but that night she told me she couldn't lie to me. 'That's Eduardo Verástegui,' she told me. I was just praying he wouldn't sit near us."

As it turned out, both Verástegui and Wolfington sat nearby.

Pons and Wolfington had a wide-ranging discussion on a variety of topics.

Midway through their conversation, Wolfington paused to say: "I have a sense that we did not sit next to each other by accident."

The next day, while talking with Verástegui and Pons, Wolfington mentioned that they were looking for someone who could help them manage and follow up with all the national organizations that were helping support *Bella*. Wolfington told Pons they were looking for someone full-time, but couldn't pay much.

On January 1, Pons began doing some outreach for Metanoia. By April, Pons had taken a full-time position with the rest of the grass-tops marketing team who were following up on the hundreds of contacts who committed to help promote the movie.

"It was my job to get the message to national leaders to mobilize people," said Pons. "We wanted to get a message of love, grace, and humility to the Ninas of the world. The Metanoia people were brilliant at that because they are people of love, grace, and humility." ■

Focus on the Family honored the *Bella* team with their Appreciation Award at the Adoption Summit. "*Bella* is a moving and inspirational movie. In a day of Hollywood's excesses, profanities, and foolishness, this sensitive film speaks eloquently of life, love, and beauty," said Dr. Dobson, who is photographed here with Verástegui.

The *Bella* Ambassadors

While there were many people who helped support *Bella* there were approximately three hundred leaders and organizations the team called "*Bella* Ambassadors." The Ambassadors were people who went above and beyond to support the movie, and the *Bella* team believes they are the reason for its success.

"We customized promotional action plans for each organization where they agreed to promote

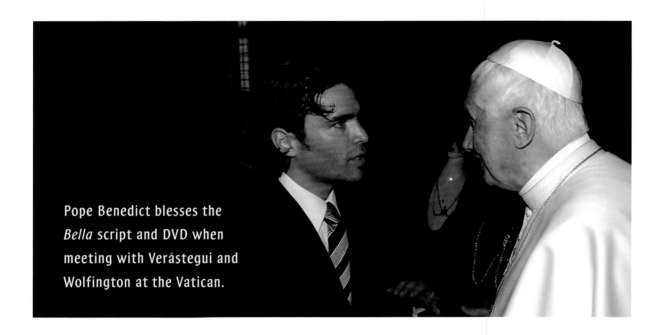

Pope Benedict blesses the *Bella* script and DVD when meeting with Verástegui and Wolfington at the Vatican.

Bella through their entire network online, offline, in their magazines, newsletters, on radio and television shows, and at their annual conferences," explained Wolfington. *Bella* received far more publicity through these organizations than through the mainstream press.

Metanoia built at least 167 coalitions with Latino groups, family groups, Christians, Catholics, pro-life organizations, and adoption groups. As a result, *Bella* was promoted by the Office of Faith Based Initiatives at the White House, Dr. James Dobson and Focus on the Family, the Family Research Council, Family Life, Bill Hybels and Willow Creek, Rick Warren and Saddleback, American Family Association, the Dove Foundation, Teen Mania, Esperanza, Salem Media, Lou Engle and the Call, EWTN, the Knights of Columbus, the U.S. Conference of Catholic Bishops, the Legionaries of Christ, Opus Dei, St. Vincent de Paul, Care Net, Heartbeat International, National Right to Life (NRL), American Life League (ALL), LifeSiteNews.com, National Council for Adoption, La Raza, LULAC, and the Hispanic Chambers of Commerce among many others.

Bella's unprecedented support came from groups that in the past have not worked together. Some of the most influential organizations in the world got behind *Bella* because they saw it as a tool to help them fulfill their mission. Focus on the Family honored the *Bella* team with their Appreciation Award at the Adoption Summit they hosted for hundreds of Christian adoption agencies, and they aggressively promoted the movie throughout their entire network.

One of *Bella*'s first screenings was at Focus on the Family. "Steve McEveety brought us there because Focus helped a lot with *The Passion of the Christ*. That's where we met Deanne Ward, an amazing woman who dedicated months of her time to connect us with everyone at Focus and with some of the biggest Christian and adoption leaders in the country," said Wolfington.

"*Bella* is a moving and inspirational movie. In a day of Hollywood's excesses, profanities and foolishness, this sensitive film speaks eloquently of life, love, and beauty," said Dr. Dobson. "It is a powerful movie that reveals the beauty of sacrificial love," added Jim Daly, President of Focus on the Family.

After watching the movie Dr. Dobson, Jim Daily, Glenn Williams, and Ken Windebank personally promoted *Bella* throughout their huge network via email, websites, magazines, and radio.

The Family Research Council also invited Verástegui and Wolfington to give a presentation at their annual conference in front of thousands of faith leaders.

Bill Hybels from Willow Creek asked Wolfington to share his story at their annual Leadership Conference, which was viewed by potentially millions of leaders in countries around the world.

At the summit Hybels said, "This is a powerful, uplifting, stirring story that will be talked about for a long, long time. This is the kind of movie you can feel free to take anybody to and people are going to have unbelievable discussions afterwards. It's got a very subtle plot twist that takes your breath away."

One of the reasons *Bella* did so well with all of these groups was because it was accessible and relevant to everyone and not just people in the Latino, faith, and adoption communities.

As word got out the team received calls and support from people they never imagined would know about *Bella*. Rick Warren, the author of *The Purpose Driven Life*, taped a personal video to send out to his network of thousands of churches and called *Bella* "the best movie of the year—everyone must see it."

Teen Mania promoted *Bella* at all their major stadium events that attract 10,000 to 40,000 teens who want to grow in their faith. After watching *Bella* president and founder Ron Luce aggressively promoted it. He challenged teens to use *Bella* as a tool to inspire the kids they knew in their hometowns.

Lou Engle from The Call was another zealous supporter who invited Verástegui to speak at his events in front of tens of thousands of youth leaders where he showed the *Bella* trailers and endorsed the movie. "Jaeson Ma introduced us to Lou and both of them shared *Bella* with hundreds of thousands of people," said Severino. Jaeson Ma volunteered to mobilize over 100,000 young leaders who are a part of his Campus Church Networks.

Bella was promoted by the Office of Faith Based Initiatives at the White House, Dr. James Dobson and Focus on the Family, the Family Research Council, Family Life, Bill Hybels and Willow Creek, Rick Warren and Saddleback, American Family Association, the Dove Foundation, Teen Mania, Esperanza, Salem Media, Lou Engle and the Call, EWTN, the Knights of Columbus, the U.S. Conference of Catholic Bishops, the Legionaries of Christ, Opus Dei, St. Vincent de Paul, Care Net, Heartbeat International, National Right to Life (NRL), American Life League (ALL), LifeSiteNews.com, National Council for Adoption, La Raza, League of United Latin American Citizens (LULAC), and the Hispanic Chambers of Commerce among many others.

Ma explained why he got involved. "*Bella* showed me the power of what a movie can do to change the heart of a generation. I got behind this movie because it was more than a movie; it was a message that every person today needed to see and hear. *Bella* changed my heart and it will continue to change the hearts and lives of those who watch it."

"While it was difficult at first for us to distribute and promote *Bella* on our own, new people continued to join our mission every week and they brought so much energy and hope that it fueled our own belief," said Verástegui.

"One day we received an email with an article written by Chuck Colson, the founder of Prison Fellowship Ministries, where he wrote eloquently about the movie and encouraged everyone to go. This is one example of the many wonderful surprises we would get on a daily basis as we were caring for *Bella*," said Severino.

Luis Cortez, the founder of Esperanza, invited the *Bella* team to his annual White House Hispanic prayer breakfast where he gave Eduardo Verástegui their prestigious Image Award and showed footage from the film.

There Verástegui met Marcos Witt, who mobilized countless people from Lakewood Church, the largest church in the country. Through Marcos the team met many other Latino pastors who got behind *Bella*. One pastor who went all out to promote the movie was Erwin McManus, who also makes films that impact culture.

Stuart and Nancy Epperson, the founders of Salem Communications, the fourth largest radio company in the U.S., gave *Bella* unprecedented support through their vast network of radio stations, websites, and magazines. "Nancy sent a letter to all their radio stations asking them to see and support *Bella*," said Verástegui.

Dick Bott from the Bott radio network also donated enormous amounts of radio promotions and granted many interviews.

Relevant Radio, founded by Mark Follett, ran free ads and did a multi-week promotion giving away $100,000 worth of tickets they bought themselves.

The Crystal Cathedral invited Eduardo, Alejandro, and his wife, Ali, on twice to share their stories with millions of people on TV.

"Every time we turned around there was another major TV or radio outlet offering to help," said Severino.

EWTN, the largest religious media organization worldwide, which reaches 140 million homes, also got behind *Bella* after many of their leaders saw the movie. Amalia Meadows, a producer at EWTN, watched the trailer after hearing about *Bella* from a college student. "My heart was captivated by the trailer and I knew I had to get involved."

Meadows showed the film to other producers and leaders at EWTN despite the inherent skepticism the network has about promoting Hollywood films. "After seeing the movie everyone wanted to promote it," said Meadows. "The entire EWTN family got behind the movie including Doug Keck, Enrique Duprat, Chris Edwards, Fernando Verano, and Raymond Arroyo."

EWTN's founder, Mother Angelica, has not been able to meet personally with people for a very long time because of poor health. But when Eduardo came to visit her, she was miraculously moved to meet with him, and their encounter was magical.

"I don't remember the last time she was able to leave her room like that," explained Meadows. "It was a miracle that mother came out," added Sister Marie St John.

"There have been many little miracles along the way, but the most beautiful to me has been the blind faith of so many people," said Wolfington. Mother Angelica put it another way: "If we are willing to do the ridiculous, God can do the miraculous."

The adoption community really embraced the movie because it was a "realistic portrayal of the struggles young women face when confronted with an unexpected pregnancy, and it shows how adoption can often be the most loving thing you can do for your child," according to Tom Atwood, the president of the National Council for Adoption. The group gave *Bella* their prestigious Excellence in Adoption Award at their annual awards gala for its honest and positive portrayal of the beauty of adoption.

Atwood explained, "One of my favorite scenes in the movie is when José asks Nina, 'Have you ever thought about adoption?'" Atwood continued, "*Bella* might get more people to think about adoption than anything else we do, so this year we decided to use it as a tool to help people see the power and beauty of adoption in a child's life."

Because of the strong support from Atwood's organization and other adoption organizations like Bethany Christian Services, the *Bella* team decided to promote the concept of people "adopting theaters."

Crisis pregnancy centers, which help young women with unexpected pregnancies, also strongly supported the movie.

"Truly, pregnancy centers have fallen in love with *Bella*," said Kristin Hansen of Care Net. "They love how it captures the heart of their work. In the character Nina's face, they see every client who walks in the doors of pregnancy centers—often scared, alone, and fearful that abortion is their only option. The story of *Bella* has the ability to reach these women with hope and positive alternatives.

"We are working to equip every pregnancy center with multiple copies of *Bella* to be able to put it into the hands of every woman who comes in for a pregnancy test," said Hansen.

Recently the filmmakers received word from a crisis pregnancy center that gave a *Bella* DVD to a young girl who had chosen to abort her child. After watching *Bella* she chose to give her child up for adoption instead.

Robert Novak wrote an article in the *Washington Post* after viewing a screening hosted by the National Council for Adoption. "It is no propaganda film but a dramatic depiction of choices facing an unmarried pregnant woman," said Novak. "Indeed, it acknowledges a woman's pain of carrying a baby to term only to give it up for adoption. In the end, however, the film is a heart-wrenching affirmation of life over death."

The film is popular in the pro-life community because it shows the value of adoption as a positive choice for a woman facing an unwanted pregnancy. In the final scene of the movie, Nina, the mother, meets her baby Bella for the first time and recognizes the significance of the choice she had made years before.

"The story is honest, non-judgmental, and real, and all types of people connected with it," said Rai Rojas from National Right to Life, a huge supporter of the film, which screened it at their national conference twice. Father Frank Pavone, head of Priests for Life, a big supporter of the film, said, "The movie helps young women make the right choice, not out of fear, but out of hope."

Juno and *Bella* both dealt with the topic of pregnancy and both characters decided for adoption over abortion. "*Bella* reminds young women who are in the same situation that they are not alone and that adoption is a beautiful choice," said Steve Jalsevac from LifeSiteNews.com, who supported the movie from the very beginning.

"The reason *Bella* was so successful is because it goes much deeper than the political slogans and emotional rhetoric some people use when discussing this topic. It told a true story that spoke to people's souls," said Tom Atwood, from the National Council for Adoption. "This little movie created an oasis where people from completely different points of view worked together to support the film's mission to celebrate the beauty of adoption."

Many organizations in the Catholic Church also aggressively supported the film because of its positive message. Erin McCrory was given the task of working with Catholic organizations.

Originally, Metanoia had been advised by many people in Hollywood to ignore Catholics. The thinking was that they typically don't collectively mobilize for anything—politics, music, or movies.

Carl Anderson (left) and Eduardo Verástegui (right) visiting the Cristeros museum in Mexico. Anderson and the Knights of Columbus gave *Bella* unprecedented support by mobilizing their local councils around the world.

McCrory, however, developed a plan focusing on Catholics and presented it to Wolfington. He liked it and supported her pursuit of the plan.

McCrory's idea involved arranging diocesan screenings of the film through the dioceses and the Knights of Columbus councils. Metanoia hoped that every diocese and Knights council, of which there are thousands, could adopt a theater and resell tickets.

In January 2007, McCrory and others from the team flew out to Washington, D.C., to connect with Carl Anderson, the leader of the Knights, and Andrew Walther, the head of communications. While there, Anderson met with Verástegui in D.C. and again in Connecticut three weeks later. The Knights agreed to promote the film and put *Bella* in all their magazines, newsletters, and websites, and Karl agreed to send out personal emails to everyone himself.

"When we realized how much they loved the movie and what they were willing to do we were so excited. It was amazing," said Severino. "Carl Anderson and Andrew Walther were part of our team. They not only promoted *Bella* everywhere but they also gave us great advice on how to mobilize the Catholic community," said Wolfington. "The Knights also created a commercial that featured Eduardo as part of their Christmas campaign to encourage people to serve the poor. It was beautiful."

"Knowing we had a lot of momentum, I asked Sean if I could have an assistant," said McCrory. "That's when we created the internship program and I got fifteen assistants."

As a result, Metanoia built an internship program that eventually included hundreds of volunteers that worked to promote the movie throughout its entire release. The internship has now grown into a year-round program dedicated to promoting positive films that can make a difference in people's lives. They have named it www.PositiveMediaResources.com and currently there are almost three hundred interns working in the program.

Eventually, almost one hundred private screenings were coordinated with Catholic leaders in the top regions in the country. McCrory was able to speak with Philadelphia's Cardinal Justin Rigali, a close friend of the Wolfingtons, who had agreed to help promote *Bella* after he saw it with Eustace Wolfington.

Cardinal Rigali not only asked the United States Conference of Catholic Bishops to cooperate with Metanoia, but also put McCrory in touch with Dierdre McQuade, director of the U.S. Bishops' secretariat. McQuade sent a letter out to the country's diocesan leaders to invite them to set up screenings of the film.

Chicago's Cardinal Francis George, Philadelphia's Cardinal Justin Rigali, and San Francisco Archbishop George Niederauer cosigned a letter to every bishop encouraging them to identify someone who could help set up a screening for local church leaders. "Cardinal Rigali promoted *Bella* in his own diocese and throughout the entire nation," said Eustace Wolfington.

McCrory asked Steve McEveety to videotape a message along with the rest of the *Bella* team to show before and after the private screenings. "The last film with *Bella*'s momentum was *The Passion of the Christ*," said McEveety. "*The Passion* showed how Christ died for us. *Bella* shows how we should live for others."

McEveety also traveled to many events with the *Bella* team to encourage people to support his first project since making *The Passion* and starting his new production company called MPower Pictures.

"Steve was one of the first people to believe in *Bella* and that meant so much to us; it helped us believe even more. He introduced us to everyone who supported *The Passion* and he came to every event we asked him to come to. He was incredibly generous and good to us," explained Wolfington.

Time was short, but in the end, approximately ninety screenings were held, with about three hundred leaders per screening. McCrory was greatly assisted by Philadelphia's Cardinal Justin Rigali, San Diego Bishop Robert Brom, and Kent Peters, director of social justice for the Diocese of San Diego. "Without them and the interns, the plan never would have been so successful," admitted McCrory.

Through a connection with an intern during these screenings, Metanoia also met up with Greg Nunn, the president of Regal Cinema, the largest theater chain in the world. Within two weeks,

Some of the more than 300 interns who work for PositiveMediaResources.com, a network of volunteers who actively promote *Bella* and other positive films. Here they are shown with Sean Wolfington (right) and Erin McCrory (left) at a private workshop that is part of an ongoing formation program for the interns.

Metanoia had set up a screening in Knoxville for Dunn and others at Regal which helped the film secure key theaters during its release. "Greg Dunn and the entire Regal theater chain were incredibly supportive of *Bella* and they gave us their best theater in New York City," said Verástegui.

Peter Brown, the head of AMC, the second largest theater chain, was also very supportive and gave *Bella* their best theater in New York also. When Cinemark came on board, the top three theater chains in the country had gotten behind *Bella*'s mission. "It was amazing that the leaders of the three largest theater chains were eager to help *Bella* because of its family friendly message and strong grass-roots support," said Severino.

"Erin did a great job creating the plan and recruiting interns to execute it," said Wolfington.

"Even though Catholics don't mobilize as quickly as Evangelicals, they had a network in place to communicate with one another and others," said McCrory. "I had never seen the Catholic Church act like that before."

The *Bella* team built coalitions with Catholic organizations ranging from various Catholic colleges and universities, to the Knights of Columbus, St. Vincent de Paul Society, Regnum Christi, Opus Dei, Legatus, and many others.

"They all set aside their differences and came together to promote the film," said McCrory. "It was great to witness." ◼

The *Bella* Magic

Between January and September 2007, the film was screened over a hundred times. Corby Pons recalled one particularly stressful screening in Texas sponsored by Governor Rick Perry.

"When I arrived in Dallas, no one knew what was going on," said Pons. "Sean's flight was delayed out of Miami. Eduardo was late, and when he did arrive he wasn't dressed for the event. We didn't have the DVD of the film or pens and surveys to collect the necessary data.

"Our supply guy got lost," said Pons. "There was absolutely no way everything was going to come together. There were seven hundred fifty people there to see the film and I felt that we were going to fail miserably."

Wolfington arrived just before Governor Perry. A FedEx truck carrying the untested DVDs arrived as the Governor arrived. After both the Governor and Wolfington spoke, the movie started.

Wolfington told Pons that they needed the survey materials. In a last ditch effort to solicit assistance, Wolfington shared the *Bella* story to one of the police officers. The officer offered to help Pons get what he needed.

"What do we have to do first?" the officer asked Pons.

"We need a thousand pens," responded Pons.

68

With the siren blaring, the police officer took Pons to a nearby Staples for pens. The store was flooded with water, so they were turned away. They headed for a neighboring Target store, where the officer helped Pons carry out the pens. Then, the officer took Pons to a Kinkos where the survey document had been emailed and copied.

"When we returned to the theater, the movie was over and Eduardo was finishing up his testimony," said Pons. "We were able to hand out our surveys and collect the information. There are similar stories from every screening of things that went wrong but still came together. We started calling it the *Bella* magic.

"The only thing better than *Bella* is the story behind *Bella*," said Pons.

At a Tampa screening, the DVDs kept skipping. The team went through seven DVDs before deciding to halt the screening.

"Still, the people were so overwhelmed with Eduardo that they signed up to pre-sell four thousand tickets," said Pons. "As Eduardo traveled the country, people were inspired by his convictions and that he was willing to pass up millions of dollars because of his beliefs."

"He travelled almost every day of the week for over a year. Either Leo or I would go with him, but he always had to be there because he is the face of *Bella*," said Wolfington. At the end of every screening, Verástegui would share his story and Metonia's mission. "And after seeing the movie and hearing Eduardo's talk, everyone wanted to get involved," added Wolfington. ▪

(From left to right) Eduardo Verástegui, Tony Bennett, Alejandro Sanz, and Sean Wolfington attend the event that celebrated *Bella* becoming the #1 rated film of 2007 (as rated by Rotten Tomatoes).

Star Power

In addition to the film's win at Toronto, *Bella* was helped along tremendously by the attention it received from the top film festivals, celebrities, and world leaders who saw the film and promoted it. They included actors Edward James Olmos, musicians Alejandro Sanz and Tony Bennett, and talk-show hosts Kathie Lee Gifford and Rosie O'Donnell, the Mexican Ambassador, and the President of the United States, among others.

Actor Edward James Olmos chose the film to open the Los Angeles Latino International Film Festival. "It is one of the most impressive landmark films to open our festival in ten years," said Olmos, "*Bella* is a film people have to see. It really captures the heart and makes you think. It is one of the best films to come out in a long time."

Bella was also selected for the Miami International Film Festival and festivals in New York, San Diego, Dallas, Austin, Santa Barbara, and Mexico. In the end *Bella* won the Heartland Film Festival's Grand Prize of $100,000, the largest festival award in the world.

Bella also won Best Picture and Best Actor from the Movieguide Awards founded by Ted Baehr. After seeing *Bella*, Baehr went above and beyond to promote the movie through his vast

The *Bella* team gathers for dinner at the Wolfington home in Miami. Pictured from left to right are Alejandro and Ali Monteverde, Jeb and Columba Bush, Sean and Ana Wolfington, and Eduardo Verástegui.

network and his film review site which is one of the top movie sites in the industry. "Ted was supportive and incredibly helpful from the very beginning," said Wolfington.

The film received several honors. The Smithsonian Latino Center presented Verástegui and Monteverde with the Legacy Award for *Bella* at its annual ¡Smithsonian Con Sabor! gala. The Legacy Award honors role models who have made a significant impact on American culture and society through their art.

"*Bella* is a masterpiece and it will be in the Smithsonian's archives along with the Hope Diamond, the Star-Spangled Banner, the flag that inspired our National Anthem, and the Ruby Slippers worn by Dorothy in *The Wizard of Oz*," said Henry Munoz, the Chairman of the Smithsonian Latino Center.

Pilar O'Leary, the previous executive director of the Center, and Munoz attended private screenings for Latino leaders across the country. "Pilar and Henry have given their life to support art that celebrates the Latino culture and values, and we cannot express how much their support helped *Bella*'s release," said Wolfington.

"We applaud Metanoia Films for their work and dedication in presenting the Latino experience in a dignified and positive light," said O'Leary at the Smithsonian screening event hosted by Columba Bush. Columba Bush is on the board of the Smithsonian, and she and her husband Jeb Bush hosted a private screening of the film in Miami to announce the award and to show the movie to top leaders in Florida. "Columba and Jeb got behind *Bella* from the very beginning and their support helped us reach all the key leaders in Florida, Washington, D.C., and across the country," said Wolfington.

In addition, Monteverde was invited to the White House to receive the Department of

"You so rarely see a movie about true, sacrificial love. We live in such a selfish generation. This movie tells the story of the laying-down-your-life kind of love," said Kathie Lee Gifford.

Verástegui and Wolfington ate lunch with Hoda Kotb (left) and Kathie Lee Gifford (center) of *The Today Show* team, as well as Tony and Susan Bennett (right of center), at the world famous Michael's Restaurant in New York City. The team discussed *The Today Show* episode that would promote *Bella*'s DVD release and the new segment they plan to produce called "Everyone Has a Story," based on the song which *Bella* inspired Kathie Lee to write.

(Top) Tony Bennett was so inspired by Eduardo and *Bella* that he asked to paint Eduardo's portrait in his art studio. In the end, Bennett made four separate paintings based on the rough depiction seen above. (Lower left) Bennett and Verástegui laughing at the Emmy Award Gala event honoring Bennett. *Bella* received the Tony Bennett "Media Excellence Award" at the event. (Lower right) Bennett spontaneously takes the mike after the world premiere of *Bella* at Tribeca and gives an impassioned speech saying, "*Bella* is a perfect film, an artistic masterpiece."

THE WHITE HOUSE

WASHINGTON

February 2, 2007

Mr. Alejandro Monteverde
3601 Holboro Drive
Los Angeles, California 90027

Dear Alejandro:

Laura and I were honored that you could join us at the Capitol for my State of the Union Address. Congratulations on the success of *Bella*. You have a very bright future in front of you.

Your extraordinary story is an example of the great promise of America, and your enterprising and determined spirit is an inspiration. I am proud to call you my fellow citizen.

Best wishes.

Sincerely,

George W. Bush

Key *Bella* supporters attended National Adoption Day at the White House with the *Bella* team. Pictured from left to right: Bob Unanue (CEO of Goya Foods), Eduardo Verástegui, Sean Wolfington, and Raymond Arroyo (EWTN).

Alejandro Monteverde (writer, director) with President and Mrs. Bush on the evening he joined the first lady in her private box to watch the state of the union address, and the day after he received the American by Choice Award from the Department of Citizenship & Immigration at a White House ceremony.

To Alejandro Monteverde
With best wishes,

Sean Wolfington, Jack Templeton, and Eduardo Verástegui at the Movieguide Awards where *Bella* won Best Picture and Verástegui won Best Actor.

Citizenship and Immigration Service's American by Choice Award, and was invited by First Lady Laura Bush to attend the State of the Union Address.

The Mexican Ambassador selected *Bella* for a special private screening at the Embassy's Cultural Institute before their exclusive Cinco de Mayo event for Hispanic world leaders and the Cinco de Mayo event at the White House the next day. "It was amazing to have the opportunity to screen the film for the most influential Latino leaders in the world and then celebrate Cinco de Mayo with them on the lawn of the White House with the most influential person in the world, the President of the United States," said Verástegui.

That would not be the last time the *Bella* team would be invited to the White House. After hearing a lot about the movie the First Lady's assistant, Lindsey Lineweaver, called Wolfington to ask if he could send a print to the White House for the First Lady and President to watch in the private White House theater.

"We could not believe that the President and First Lady wanted to see our little movie. It was surreal," said Wolfington. "I called the amigos and said, 'you are not going to believe what I am about to tell you,' but then again, that was the lead in to many of the conversations we had over that year."

After seeing the film, the White House invited Verástegui to give the keynote speech on National Adoption Day. "I was so nervous because I had to address approximately three hundred of the most knowledgeable adoption leaders in the country who knew more about adoption than I did," explained Verástegui.

"Eduardo was very intimidated, but when he got up there he spoke from the heart and received a standing ovation at the end. He gave a beautiful talk that brought many people to tears, including me," said Wolfington.

President Bush's adopted niece, Marshall Bush, saw *Bella* and fell in love with the story. She became a zealous supporter because of its pro-adoption theme. Marshall Bush explained, "The story shows what adoption can do for a child, and it has inspired many people to adopt children. What is more beautiful than that?"

Bush volunteered to promote *Bella* and set up a website with her best friend Morgan Kondash to get the word out. Kondash decided to work full-time with *Bella*, and Marshall Bush was also happy to celebrate the fact that the *Bella* team received the President's Volunteer and Service award for their contribution to their service to the community.

Multi-award winning Grammy artist Alejandro Sanz was so taken by the film that he offered two songs from his best-selling album, *El tren de los momentos*, for the movie. Sanz actually remade one of his most popular songs, "En la planta de tus pies," for the movie, and he told his fans to go to the film during his sold-out concert tour that happened to correspond with *Bella*'s theatrical release. Jon Foreman, the lead singer of the band Switchfoot, also offered a song after being inspired by the film.

"He gave us his favorite song that he wrote for his wife when they were dating," said Wolfington. "It's so personal that he said he probably won't include it on his first solo CD, but he gave it to us for our movie." Michael W. Smith, another very popular musician, zealously promoted *Bella* on his website as did Jars of Clay.

Talk-show host Rosie O'Donnell unexpectedly named the film one of her favorites of 2007, and she encouraged people to see the movie when she appeared on *The Today Show*.

The film received some of its best endorsements from Kathie Lee Gifford and Tony Bennett. Gifford was introduced to the film through a friend, Emilie Weirda, in the Florida Keys.

"Just before Thanksgiving, Emilie called saying, 'Please tell me you're coming down to Florida. We're having a screening for a film I know you'll love.'"

But Gifford had just had surgery on her feet and was unable to travel.

"Emilie asked if it would be okay if she had the producer call me for a screening in Greenwich. I spoke to Sean Wolfington on Friday, and he and Eduardo were at my home by Sunday for a screening for twenty to thirty people," said Gifford.

"I was deeply moved by the film," said Gifford. "I asked them what I could do to help them promote it, and I told them if they stayed in town a few days I might be able to get some publicity for it."

Verástegui and Wolfington stayed with the Giffords for four days. It was through Gifford that Verástegui was able to secure an interview on *Entertainment Tonight*. ◼

"Everyone Has a Story"

The film also inspired Gifford to write and record a song, "Everyone Has a Story." The song's lyrics talk about the central theme of *Bella*—that there comes a time in all our lives when something happens that changes us forever and we will never be the same again. It reminds us that "everyone has a story" and that we cannot judge people because we often don't know people's entire story. If we did we would probably have compassion rather than being judgmental.

"You so rarely see a movie about true, sacrificial love," said Gifford. "We live in such a selfish generation. This movie tells the story of the laying-down-your-life kind of love."

Gifford recalled her father telling her to "give, give, give."

"How will I know when I've given enough?" she would ask her Dad.

"When it costs you something," was his reply. "When it hurts."

Gifford sees *Bella* as a pro-adoption movie that has already inspired countless people to adopt.

"It's a powerful message gently told," said Gifford.

After promoting *Bella*, Gifford was asked to join *The Today Show* and she agreed. When she had been there only two months, the ratings for the show shot up by fourteen points, the highest increase in the show's ratings in the history of her part of the show.

Gifford invited Verástegui on the show and did a ten-day countdown to a fantastic segment that lasted much longer than most. Gifford pitched producers the idea of doing a segment on Eduardo's story and she wanted Eduardo to sing, "Everyone Has a Story," the song *Bella* inspired her to write.

The producers loved the idea so much they agreed to do a special series of segments called "Everyone has a story" to go on beyond Eduardo's episode. Unfortunately, Verástegui was not able to learn the song in time and the producers eventually convinced Kathie Lee to sing the song herself since she wrote it.

The Today Show is launching this new series called "Everyone Has a Story" in September when this book comes out and they are using the song as the theme for the new segment.

Everyone Has a Story

by Kathie Lee Gifford & David Friedman

Everyone has a story
Different as night and day
And everyone has their own Journey
Some follow their path, some wander away

But everyone has a moment
That changes their life, and then
It's suddenly clear in that moment
That nothing will ever be the same again

> *Careful, the plans we make*
> *Careful, the roads we take*
> *Careful, the hearts we break*
> *Along the way*

> *Careful, the things embraced*
> *Careful, the time we waste*
> *Careful, the dreams we taste*
> *And toss away*

Everyone has a purpose
Different as day and night
And everyone finds their own answer
Some blinded by fear, some guided by light

Yes, everyone has a story
A beginning, a middle and end
But if there's a God in the heavens above
And if there's such a thing as a thing called love
Then there must be a way for anyone's heart to mend

> *Careful, the chance we take*
> *Careful, the choice we make*
> *Careful, for heaven's sake*
> *The road we take*

Everyone has a story

"Who would have guessed that Kathie Lee Gifford would fall in love with *Bella* and promote it the way she has? We received more positive feedback from that show than any other publicity, Kathie has been a guardian angel to us," said Wolfington. "Just the other day she emailed me to let me know that she spoke with the president of Wal-Mart and Universal music about *Bella* and that they are going to watch it this weekend. She has been amazing."

Through Wolfington's twin brother Ryan, Metanoia was able to invite Tony Bennett to the film's New York premiere. After the film, Bennett spontaneously took to the stage to describe the film as a "rare work of art, a perfect movie, and a masterpiece.

"This film," he continued, "is an artistic masterpiece that every American must see! To create something at this level is nearly impossible and these young guys did it. The timing, cinematography, and music are amazing. *Bella* is timeless and made for this time in our country when Mexicans and Americans are divided. This movie builds bridges of healing and reminds everyone of what's most important in life."

The film was awarded the Tony Bennett Media Excellence Award at an Emmy award gala honoring Tony's career. Bennett compared Eduardo to Sidney Poitier because they both shared a mission to make movies that portrayed their culture in a more honest and positive light.

Tony was so inspired by Eduardo and the film that he painted a portrait of Eduardo in his studio overlooking central park. No amateur painter, Bennett also has a picture in the Smithsonian Institute. "Tony has been incredibly kind and generous to us and has become a lifelong friend," said Verástegui. ◼

Sean Wolfington, Frank and Kathie Lee Gifford, and Eduardo Verástegui at a private screening of *Bella* for family and friends hosted by the Giffords in their home theater.

The Obstacles to Getting a Distributor

After deciding to release the movie on their own, the *Bella* team needed to find the right distributor to rent their system. Despite all the progress *Bella* was making, the team had yet to find a suitable distribution partner. The first opportunity came through attorney John Jakubczyk. When he first saw *Bella*, the film resonated with him.

"If we could make a difference in one person's life through the film, it was worth it," said Jakubczyk. "*Bella* is about a man being heroic in a quiet manner—just being a friend," he added. "Sometimes *just being* there is what you need to do to make a difference."

The next month, one of Jakubczyk's new employees, a woman by the name of Melanie Welch, called him on a Friday morning.

"She called to tell me that she had seen this great film—*Bella*," said Jakubczyk. "Furthermore, she said that her roommate, Brooke Burns, had an uncle, Michael Burns, who is the vice chairman of the film studio and distributor Lionsgate.

"Well, what's she doing this weekend?" Jakubczyk asked. "Show her the film."

Burns had a bridal shower, but was free after that. Jakubczyk arranged a flight for Burns from Phoenix to Los Angeles where they set up a showing of the film at Monteverde's home.

"Burns loved it and made the arrangements for her uncle to see it," said Jakubczyk.

The road to distribution, however, would wind on for several more months. Despite the fact that Michael Burns loved the film, his team passed on it because they did not believe it was marketable.

By January 2007, members of the team had screened *Bella* with practically every group that aligned with the film. Despite *Bella*'s strong support from so many quarters, Metanoia still could not get a distributor who was willing to finance any part of the release of the movie. As a result, the Wolfingtons continued to finance the entire P & A budget budget until the *Bella* team met a few generous men who would help support the rest. ◾

A Few
Generous
Men

Jason Jones, vice president of Sovereign City, a radio content company based in Green Bay, introduced the Metanoia team to some investors from Green Bay who were interested in helping out.

Jones encountered the film in the beginning of 2006 while attending a conference in Mexico City. A friend of Jones' knew Eduardo, Leo, and Sean and asked if he wanted to go see the film.

"I didn't want to go," said Jones. "I had been stuck in traffic for hours and it was late. New Jersey Congressman Chris Smith's wife grabbed me by the earlobe and said, 'You're going to go.'"

At the theater it was hot. One of the people asked if anyone needed water.

Jones offered to help get water, never guessing that the person he was filling up Dixie cups with was Sean Wolfington, the film's financier and producer.

Hot and tired, Jones was looking forward to the movie because he figured he could get some sleep. He planned to slink into the theater chair for some much needed rest.

"As soon as the movie started it grabbed my attention and all I could think was that I was seeing one of the most beautiful movies ever made and I was seeing it before anyone else."

Jones' connection to the film was personal.

At the age of seventeen, Jones learned that his girlfriend was expecting. As a result, Jones dropped out of high school and joined the Army. He and his girlfriend intended to tell her parents following basic training at Fort Benning, Georgia. The girl's mother became suspicious, her parents learned the truth, and her father physically assaulted her. A friend of her father's took her to an abortion business where the baby girl was aborted.

"I was devastated. Our child was gone and we could not do anything about it. I promised my girlfriend and my child that I would never let something like that ever happen again. Promoting this film is part of how I am trying to live up to that promise.

"Based on my own experience, seeing how Nina suffered alone, I felt how my ex-girlfriend suffered alone," said Jones. "I realized that this film could have a tremendous impact on how people think about the dignity of the mother and the child. That's the whole focus of the film and that's what I loved about it."

After seeing the film, Jones received a call from Wolfington who invited him to attend a screening at Notre Dame the next week. He flew out and met the whole team. After that weekend he was moved to call Wolfington. Jones ended up introducing the *Bella* team to some of the folks—Mark Follett, Bob Atwell, and David Hackney—who helped provide the other half of the funding for the P & A needed to release the movie.

Jones called Atwell saying, "You've got to meet these guys."

It wasn't until months later, after *Bella* won in Toronto, that Follett, Atwell, and Hackney finally saw the film at a screening in Green Bay. In the fall of 2006, they met the *Bella* team in Miami and committed the other half of the money for the promotion and distribution of the film.

"They needed money to get exposure for the film after it had been made, but before its theatrical release," explained Atwell. "We signed on because we believed in the mission."

"An investment advisor never would have advised getting involved in the film," admitted Atwell. "It was high-risk without the promise of a return, but we knew it could make a huge impact on people's lives."

After the movie was released, Fred and Ken Foote were similarly moved by the film and offered to invest in the P & A budget, as was another entrepreneur named Brad Reeves. Collectively, their investment was used to continue the ongoing promotion of *Bella*.

"Fred and Ken's investment came at a time when we had to decide if we could continue to expand the release of the movie. Because of them we were able to increase the number of theaters and the impact. We were overwhelmed by their generosity," said Wolfington.

Fred Foote, who operates the Heritage Mark Foundation, first saw the film after its Toronto win. He viewed it in the offices of Steve McEveety while in Hollywood to look at films that were seeking investors.

"I had seen a film earlier in the day that didn't impress me," said Foote. "*Bella* was the kind of film that could make a difference."

Foote described the film as the rare sort of thing that comes out of Hollywood that he felt was worthy to show your teenage daughter.

"*Bella* was about an act of love motivated by a person in love with the Lord and other people," said Foote. Brad Reeves also offered to support the film after he saw the impact the movie was having on people everywhere. ■

Bella Goes
Down the Aisle

Monteverde described the time trying to find a distributor as the low point. "We feared the film would never hit theaters," said Monteverde. "It was very discouraging.

"It was a year of distributors playing with us," said Monteverde. "We would begin talks with a distributor. They would say they were going to get back to us and then we wouldn't hear anything. Those we did hear back from offered deals that were bad for us."

Undeterred, the *Bella* team moved forward with their grass-roots promotion, traveling the country to host screenings and talk about the film with those who could support it.

Metanoia's marketing strategy focused on two objectives. One was to get organizations to help promote the film. The other was to get organizations to pre-purchase tickets, show times, and DVDs.

"We travelled for months promoting the movie while we looked for the right distributor to book the theaters," said Monteverde. "We kept working in faith."

The team knew there was an audience for the film. At the screenings, audiences enjoyed it, so they knew that eventually they would find the right distributor.

Distribution didn't come easily. The Metanoia team faced a series of false starts in January, April, May, July, and August. Originally, Lionsgate passed on the film, and the *Bella* team began working with a smaller company that handled independent films. Eventually, that deal fell through as well.

Finding a distributor was complicated by the nature of the film. The distributors liked it, but didn't know how to market it.

"They weren't very passionate about it," said Monteverde.

Near the end, Wolfington returned to Lionsgate because he knew they were one of the best distributors in the industry. Wolfington called Michael Burns of Lionsgate,

Bella wins Movieguide's Best Picture Award and Verástegui gets Best Actor Award. Pictured from left to right: Eduardo Verástegui, Ted Beahr (founder of Movieguide), and Sean Wolfington.

and told him, "We are getting ready to walk down the aisle with another distributor, but we wanted to see if we might be able to marry our first love before we said, 'I do,'" said Verástegui.

In the end, the *Bella* team made an arrangement with Lionsgate's partner, Roadside Attractions, to rent their distribution system for the theatrical release while using Lionsgate for the DVD and other ancillary markets—television, cable, airlines, universities, etc.

"The film is a crowd pleaser about humanity, family, friendship, and the unique magic of New York City," Eric d'Arbeloff, co-president of Roadside, told the *Hollywood Reporter*. "*Bella* won the hearts and minds of Latino and mainstream audiences alike, and it found the same success as previous Toronto People's Choice Award winners *Life Is Beautiful*, *Whale Rider*, and *Hotel Rwanda*."

Despite being much smaller than the giant films released during Thanksgiving and Christmas, the movie did exceptionally well, staying in theaters for twenty-six weeks. "A film is fortunate to be in the theaters for four to six weeks these days. Because there are fewer theaters than films made they have to rotate movies quickly, but *Bella* defied the odds," said John Logigian, a Hollywood veteran executive. ▪

Getting the Word Out

Publicity was a big part of the *Bella* team's strategy to get the word out about the movie. "We needed publicists for the general, faith, and Latino markets," explained Wolfington. "We got the most publicity from the Spanish media thanks to our publicity team from Latin World Entertainment (LWE) in Miami."

"Witnessing the conception, development, and birth of *Bella* brought so much love to all of those that worked on it that we ended up adopting the project as if it were our own," said Melissa Balaguer of LWE. The energy and the magic that *Bella* exuded were so contagious that it became an LWE child. Employees from all departments ended up volunteering to pamper and feed it 24/7.

"*Bella* will always mark a sweet part of our company's history. It brought a proud smile to all of us, the same way parents celebrate their kids' achievements as they mature, never wanting to let go completely," Balaguer concluded.

"Luis, Melissa, Conchita, and the entire team became a part of our family," said Verástegui. "Conchita and the team did such a good job that I was always talking to someone they'd encouraged to promote *Bella*."

The team used the top Entertainment PR firm BNC for their general publicity and Bob Angelotti for their faith outreach. "Bob did all the publicity for *The Passion* and he did an amazing job on *Bella* because he knows everyone," said Wolfington. Angelotti was successful in getting *Bella* on all the big Christian and conservative TV and radio shows including

the biggest of them all, Rush Limbaugh's show, which reaches over twenty million people.

"*Bella* was unlike any other film I have ever worked on, because it was much more than a movie. It was a movement—a movement supported by people from all walks of life and ethnic backgrounds who believed passionately in the beauty of life, family, and true friendship that *Bella* so powerfully portrayed on film."

Now the difficult job was to coordinate and communicate with all of these publicity companies, the producers, and the actors. This job was filled by Ted Royer. Ted Royer first saw *Bella* at the South by Southwest Film Festival in Austin, Texas, in mid-March of 2007. Royer had spent the previous decade working in politics. Both he and the film's director had attended the same church in Austin for a time.

When Royer first saw the film he was a spokesman and speechwriter for Texas Governor Rick Perry. Several weeks later, Governor Perry approached Royer and asked him if he had ever heard of the film *Bella*.

Royer told Governor Perry that he had recently seen it and was wondering why the governor was asking about it.

"Yeah, I know the director. I saw it at the film festival. You'd love the message. Why are you asking me about some small independent film?" asked Royer.

"Jeb Bush called me and said I need to see this movie and take a call from the producers to see if there's a way I can help them," replied Governor Perry.

"You can get behind this," counseled Royer. "It has a positive message about Latino culture, life, adoption—all things you're passionate about."

As a result, Governor Perry took a call from Wolfington and set up a May screening for a variety of folks including state representatives as well as adoption, Latino, and faith groups. Royer went to see the film as well, this time taking his wife, Mylinda.

"It was awesome," said Royer. "Everyone was impressed with their passion and mission."

After the screening Royer spent about five minutes speaking with Wolfington and the two traded business cards.

"If you're coming back to Texas for grass-roots promotion, I have a pretty extensive media contact list," Royer told Wolfington. "I'd be happy to help however I can."

At the time, Royer was considering a dream job as a speechwriter for the CEO of a Fortune 500 company. He and his wife Mylinda, an actress, were about three weeks out from a move to Los Angeles. When Royer got to work the next day, there was a message on his voice mail from Wolfington. The two played phone tag, until Wolfington's assistant told Royer to call at exactly 2:30 P.M. and that Wolfington would be expecting the call.

There comes a time in all our lives when something happens that changes us forever and we will never be the same again.

Eduardo Verástegui, Governor Rick Perry, Alejandro Monteverde, and Sean Wolfington attend the private screening hosted by the Governor of Texas at the capital in Austin.

"All day, I felt like I needed to talk to Sean, but I didn't know why," said Royer. "I knew it was going to be an important call."

Five minutes before he was supposed to talk to Wolfington, the recruiter Royer had been talking with called about the speechwriter position.

"It was exactly what I wanted," said Royer. "Fewer hours, three times the pay. It was my plan."

Still, when the recruiter called, Royer knew that Wolfington would be calling. When the recruiter asked if it was a good time to talk, Royer said that it wasn't and that he would have to call him back.

"I knew right then that my life would probably never be the same after that," said Royer.

When Royer reached Wolfington, the first words out of Wolfington's mouth were: "Listen, I'm a go-with-my-gut kind of guy and my gut says that we need you to move to Los Angeles to run our publicity operations," recalled Royer. "The second words out of his mouth were: 'We're low budget and can't pay you anything until we open in theaters five or six months from now.'"

"I'm a go-with-my-gut kind of guy, too," Royer responded. "Obviously, I need to talk with my wife about this, but I'm about 98 percent sure I'm going to do this."

Mylinda had unexpectedly called him earlier during the day.

"She told me, 'I know I've been harping on you to get a job, but whatever God wants you to do, I'm good with,'" said Royer. "That happened three hours before I talked with Sean. It was like God took care of her heart before the offer was on the table."

Royer ended up setting up four Texas grass-roots screenings hosted by Governor Perry in Austin, Dallas, Houston, and San Antonio. After that, Royer and his wife packed everything they owned into a U-Haul truck and moved to Los Angeles.

Royer's responsibility was working with all the public relations agencies Metanoia hired to get press coverage for the film.

"Our theatrical campaign was a big challenge," admitted Royer. "We were pitching a movie that the vast majority of people had never heard of, with stars they had never heard of, and a story that's difficult to explain in a single sentence without giving everything away."

Royer admitted that the move was a huge leap of faith.

"You don't always have to be certain of the path before you," said Royer. "You can be certain of the God who is leading you."

Right before their move, a church in Austin invited Mylinda to do a question-and-answer session at a Wednesday service on the entertainment industry. While there, members of the church asked how they could pray for her.

"They prayed that we would come to Hollywood and be in contact with, and be able to work with, other Christians in the industry who had a vision for doing quality work that had a positive message," said Royer. "Just weeks after that, the prayers were answered.

"Before Sean's call, I didn't feel like I had a clear direction from God about where I was supposed to go or what I was supposed to do," said Royer. "When Sean called it was an obvious answer to prayer."

The first time Royer saw the film he liked it and was proud and happy for Monteverde.

"I didn't think beyond that," said Royer.

It wasn't until the private screening with Governor Perry that the true impact of the film hit Royer.

"I realized these guys were more than filmmakers," said Royer. "They really wanted to use their talents to impact people to the degree that a film can shape people's lives for the better."

Royer coordinated and scheduled hundreds of PR opportunities, managed the calendar and the talents' schedules, and also helped craft the messaging. "Ted passed up on huge opportunities to work for nothing, and he was one of the most important people on our team. He is an incredible writer and he knows how to manage hundreds of PR activities at once with patience and grace," said Wolfington.

Like Royer there were a few other highly skilled people who passed up big money to volunteer full-time to help *Bella* succeed. Trey Bowles called the team after seeing *Bella* and said, "I can host a screening for the most influential leaders in Dallas and other key cities in Texas," recalls Wolfington. "Trey and his team put together one of the best screenings we ever had with more than eight hundred people and a first class reception in only a few weeks."

Mitch Hesley, a Harvard business grad, worked with Severino and Wolfington to refine *Bella*'s grass-roots strategy to increase its effectiveness and impact. "Mitch is brilliant and his generosity and help were invaluable," said Severino.

"It was inspiring for me to work with so many people who came together for the common good," said Hesley.

Eduardo Gil was another talented leader who donated his summer to help Erin McCrory and Wolfington mobilize hundreds of volunteers to promote *Bella* online and beyond. "Something like *Bella* does not come along often, and I knew I had to give whatever I had to offer. It was an honor and a blessing for me," said Gil.

Kim Stryker and Lori Wahlers also stepped forward to help *Bella* reach more people because of its life changing message. "I believed so strongly in *Bella*'s mission and values, and I felt like it was my responsibility and honor to do whatever I could get the word out to as many people as possible," said Wahlers.

"Kim called out of nowhere to offer her help and one of the many things she did was introduce us to Lori, who was incredibly helpful," said Wolfington. Wahlers single-handedly convinced over a thousand radio stations across the country to run special week-long promotions to market *Bella*'s DVD.

What is it that could bring all of these people together to work for free? By now you can see that *Bella* is not just another movie. "There is something special about *Bella* that brought out the best in people who saw it and it has been amazing to witness their incredible generosity," said Verástegui.

Another generous supporter was Dino Vlahakis, co-owner with his sister Elaine, of the Pickwick Theater in the Chicago area. Dino started working in this old classic theater as a child and eventually bought it to protect it from being destroyed. Dino personally took out his own ads for *Bella* before even meeting any of the filmmakers. Jason Jones happened to stop in the theater and discovered his random act of kindness and support. The best part is that Mark Follett then decided to buy all the tickets for that weekend to give to underprivileged kids. ■

Thanks to the People,
Bella Comes to Theaters

When *Bella* opened on October 26, 2007, it was one of the few family-friendly movies being offered amid the Halloween horror flicks. Wolfington described it as a "candle amid the darkness" because *Bella* came out on the same weekend as *Saw IV* and *Before the Devil Knows You're Dead*.

In the weeks leading up to the film's October 26th opening, hundreds of groups and individuals adopted theaters and pre-purchased thousands of tickets. Because of the people's support *Bella* surprised the industry with a huge opening weekend. The film earned the second highest per-screen average of any film in theaters that weekend (more than $8,000 per-screen), even topping such films as *Forrest Gump*, *Return of the Jedi*, and *Braveheart*. *Bella* grossed $1.3 million on opening weekend on only 165 screens. Overall, the film's domestic gross was just over $8 million, which does not include any other ancillary revenue. The film remained in some theaters for as long as twenty-six weeks.

Bella was the #1 rated movie by the *New York Times* Readers Poll and by the users of Yahoo and Fandango, two of the biggest websites in the world. The film's most impressive achievement was that *Bella* was voted the #1 top rated movie of 2007, above every film released that year, by the users of the largest film review site in the world, www.RottenTomatoes.com.

Bella's success was due to the overwhelming support it received from influential leaders and organizations who used the film to impact the culture in a positive way.

"We thought things would calm down after the domestic distribution, but it's become very labor intensive," said Severino. The filmmakers organized similar grass-roots teams in Australia, Canada, Mexico, and Spain, where they hoped to recreate the same success that the film enjoyed in the U.S. The film opened in those markets just before its DVD release in the U.S. "It is great to get letters and emails from all over the world from people about how *Bella* impacted their lives," said Verástegui.

The DVD, which was released on May 6, 2008, had strong preorder sales the weekend before its release, making it the number one selling romantic movie on Amazon for the first four weeks of its release on DVD up to the writing of this book. *Bella* has also been voted the #6 top rated movie of all time on Yahoo.com, the largest website in the world. "The most important outcome for all of us has been the positive impact that *Bella* has had on people's lives," explained Eustace Wolfington. ■

The Secret to
Bella's Success

The selfless support of *Bella*'s fans and volunteers was the secret to its success. The grass-roots promotional efforts paid off in remarkable ways because close to five hundred people pre-purchased entire show times of the film on opening weekend which guaranteed a successful opening. The organizations that committed to promote *Bella* delivered beyond what was promised and thousands of people were mobilized to vote for *Bella* at the Box Office on opening weekend.

In the Dallas area, for example, more showings were sold out than anywhere else in the country, mostly through the work of a volunteer, Karen Garnett. Like so many other connections that were made, Garnett and the *Bella* team came together through other people who were supporting the movie's mission.

Garnett first met The Three Amigos through Tarek Saab, the author and speaker who

appeared on the fifth season of Donald Trump's reality show, *The Apprentice*. Saab is the CEO and co-founder of Lionheart Apparel, a Christian men's clothing designer.

Saab told Garnett that she needed to see *Bella* and that she would love the film's life-affirming theme. In October 2006, Saab invited her to a screening of the film taking place at the home of Lee Roy Mitchell, the founder of Cinemark Theaters.

"Lee Roy was supportive from the start. He understood that we were trying to tell stories that could positively impact the world, and he offered to help before he even saw the movie," said Verástegui. There, at the full-size theater in Mitchell's Dallas home, Garnett was introduced to the *Bella* team.

"As soon as I saw it, I knew that I needed to be part of the *Bella* mission," said Garnett. "The fire was lit."

Garnett became one of the film's many cheerleaders. She helped to arrange a screening for the U.S. Catholic Bishops at a Dallas conference during the summer of 2007. In the midst of it all, Garnett's mother was diagnosed with terminal cancer and passed away. Garnett was moved by Eduardo telling her how much *Bella* needed her mother's prayers. "We have another friend in heaven praying for *Bella*," she recalled him telling her.

When the movie was released Garnett partnered with various groups in Dallas to sell out most of the screenings on opening weekend. Garnett's mega-*Bella* blitz resulted in thirteen sold-out screenings in the Dallas area.

Sean, Eduardo, and Alejandro were so impressed by the Dallas efforts that they flew down to Texas after the film's New York premiere for a red-carpet event hosted by George Bush, Jr. (Jeb and Columba Bush's son) at the Cinemark 17 Theater and spoke to audiences after all of the sold-out showings.

As a result, Dallas tied New York for the opening weekend gross for the film. Over the next several weeks the film went from three theaters in Dallas to several, remaining in theaters deep into the next year. Garnett was one of many people who were deeply affected by *Bella* but also had a huge affect on the film's success.

While Garnett's story is special, it is like so many stories of people coming out of the woodwork to help this little film make a big impact. Zip Rzeppa from the St. Louis Society of St. Vincent de Paul adopted over two dozen screenings and helped Eduardo get on Bill O'Reilly's show along with Steve McEveety. O'Reilly loved the movie so much he decided to promote the DVD when it came out by putting the makers of *Bella* in his Patriot or Pinhead episode, as patriots of course.

Another person who contributed to *Bella*'s success in an extraordinary way is Bob Unanue, President of Goya Foods, Inc., the nation's largest Hispanic-owned food company. Goya sponsored *Bella*'s premieres in Miami and New York and decided to change their 60-second radio ads throughout the country to promote *Bella* during the month of the release.

After attending the premiere of *Bella* in the Miami and Tribeca film festivals, the Unanue family was so inspired by the film that they wanted to buy thousands of tickets for underprivileged Latinos who may otherwise not have an opportunity to see the movie.

"At the last minute Bob and his family agreed to buy $50,000 worth of tickets to hand out to people who could not afford them," said Wolfington. "It was amazing because they did not want anyone to know about it and they did not want any publicity for doing it." The Goya family helped organize teams of people who gave tickets out to anyone who wanted them.

Ryan Wolfington volunteered to fly to New York with Jason Jones to help the team of people who were handing out tickets. There he met a young lady named Marline.

"I ran into a group of Latino kids. I offered them tickets and told them *Bella* was a film where the Latino lead actor was a hero and not a thug like what is often portrayed in films. They said they wanted to see *Saw IV*, but I offered them an opportunity to see a story that would inspire them. They cursed the idea—and me—but one girl in the crowd apologized and promised she would return the following day to see the movie," said Wolfington.

The next day Marline returned to see *Bella* as promised. After the movie ended Wolfington explained to her the effects the wrong friends and films can have on her future. "Who you are is deeply influenced by who your friends are and by what you put in your head, through films or anything else."

The young lady was eager to learn, so Wolfington also told her ten things she could do to improve her life. He promised her that if she did all ten things he would accept her into an internship the following summer.

Two days later Marline called to tell Wolfington she'd put all ten items on a poster in her room and that she was taking action to change her life. He asked her to bring the poster the following day to meet up with Eduardo and him.

That same morning Eduardo and Ryan were meeting Bob Unanue to discuss the ticket campaign Goya financed and they shared many stories with Bob, including the story about Marline. At that moment she showed up with the poster. When Bob saw it he was so inspired that he decided they wanted to sponsor all the major Latino markets including New York, Chicago, Miami, Los Angeles and others.

In the end, Goya purchased close to $300,000 in tickets, and the stories of their impact are endless. As for Marline, she was hired by Goya and still works with them today. She is also currently working with the internship Wolfington promised and has completely turned her life around.

This is one of many stories about how the selfless generosity of those who supported *Bella* has changed the lives of countless people. Many other people heard about Goya's generosity and were inspired to donate money for the purchase of more tickets to help the program reach more kids in cities around the country.

One example is Terrance and Barbara Caster who heard about the impact the movie was having and were interested in possibly making a donation to buy tickets. The Casters founded A-1 Self Storage and are known for their generous non-profit organization called Helping Hands that helps the poor in Mexico and beyond.

"Mr. Caster told me they would go see the movie at a matinee that afternoon and then they would determine if and how they might help," said Erin McCrory. "Three hours later they called and agreed to donate the money to buy the tickets for people who could not afford them." In the end, the Casters bought $100,000 worth of tickets that were distributed in their hometown of San Diego and other key cities around the country.

Many other generous people also contributed including Doug Brown, Bernadette Neal, Brian O'Neill, Eustace Mita, Jim McGuire, Tony Hayden, Mike Barton, Tom Nerney, Dan Pollett, Carlos Alfonso, John Devaney, and Foster Friess. O'Neill hosted two giant premieres of the film in Philadelphia with a first class red-carpet treatment and reception where he invited influential leaders that could help support the film's release.

Jason Jones single-handedly raised thousands of dollars and secured invaluable promotional support from his many friends including Mark Follett and Relevant Radio who donated another $100,000 in tickets to give out to at risk teens and high school kids throughout the country.

"Mark Follett and Sean Wolfington have committed to buying $50,000 worth of DVDs to hand out to women who are dealing with newly discovered unwanted pregnancies so they know they are not alone," said Jones, who founded a non-profit organization that is equipping pregnancy centers with *Bella* DVDs.

The friends and families of the filmmakers also rallied behind *Bella* in an unbelievable way. Many of Eduardo's family members moved to LA to help out. Alejandro's and Ali's families and Leo Severino's family and extended family through the youth groups he led years before pitched in.

The entire Wolfington clan came out in droves including Alex Wolfington, Ryan Wolfington, and Marty Gillin, Eustace Wolfington's sister. They worked tirelessly along with so many other people to help little *Bella* make something of itself.

"So many people were deeply affected by *Bella*, especially those of us that had the privilege of helping to bring it to the public. I don't think we will ever know the full impact it had on people's lives," said Marty Gillin.

"None of the people who helped out asked for anything in return, not even a free DVD," said Wolfington. In the end, these generous people donated close to $500,000 to buy tickets for people who could not afford them. "The spirit of generosity that José's character conveys is what makes the movie so beautiful, and that same spirit moved these generous people to buy tickets for people they do not know," said Monteverde. ◼

Bella's successful theatrical release earned it
a full scale DVD release through Lionsgate.

Act III
new life

bella

FROM THE SCRIPT...

EXT. BEACH. DAY.

José ties Bella's shoes, as she laughs.

BELLA

Perfect.

José ties the blue scarf around her head.

JOSÉ

Wow!

(he whistles)

BELLA

How do I look?

JOSÉ

You look beautiful.

The two sit on the wall, as the taxi pulls up, carrying Nina.

Nina gets out of the taxi, smiling and crying.

Bella looks up at José and smiles, then looks back at her mother.

Nina approaches Bella.

NINA

Do you know who I am?

BELLA

You're my mama.

Nina sobs and laughs, overcome with joy and emotion.

She opens her backpack and pulls out the teddy bear, his arm stitched together with coarse red string.

Act III
new life

Monteverde said he did not set out to intentionally make a pro-adoption film.

"I told a pro-love story," said Monteverde. "Those who were involved with many different types of organizations saw the story as an answer to their prayers and promoted it."

Neither he nor anyone else connected with *Bella* expected the film's eventual outcome or eternal consequences. *Bella* had a profound impact not only on the lives of those involved with the film, but also on those who saw it.

For director Alejandro Monteverde, the film is about far more than success at the box office. He said that the movie represents life itself, in more ways than one.

"When I was writing *Bella*, I met my girlfriend," said Monteverde. "When I was shooting *Bella*, I got engaged. When I finished *Bella*, I got married, and prior to its release, we had our first baby."

Monteverde met his future wife, actress Ali Landry, through Eduardo Verástegui and Leo Severino.

"Leo was teaching his Going Deeper class for celebrities, actors, and directors in Hollywood," explained Monteverde. "She was invited and we met there."

The two connected right away. Landry had a passion for all things Spanish.

While the film was in production, Landry decided she wanted to learn Spanish. Monteverde invited her to the Spanish colonial Mexican town of San Miguel de Allende, where she ended up renting an apartment with Monteverde's parents while she was taking a month-long course in conversational Spanish.

"She kept wanting me to come down to spend a weekend," said Monteverde. "I didn't want

Alejandro Monteverde proposes to his future wife with the help of a Mariachi band in San Miguel, Mexico.

to go then because I had a plan to propose to her there later. So I told her that it was the most important time for *Bella* and there was no way, no way, no way that I could come down."

Three days before Landry was to finish her studies, she called Monteverde to ask if he was going to come down to surprise her.

"No, I'm leaving tomorrow for Miami to promote the film," Monteverde told her. "But I'm sending you a package."

That day, unbeknownst to Landry, Monteverde flew down to San Miguel and enlisted the help of his parents. Upon arrival, he gave the package to his mother. It had stamps on it, so it looked as if it had been mailed. Monteverde's mother gave the package to Landry. Inside was a video of Monteverde and Landry's relationship set to Landry's favorite music. Landry watched the video and cried.

Then Monteverde's mother took Landry to dinner at La Capilla—a four-hundred-year-old chapel that had been turned into a restaurant.

Meanwhile, Monteverde's father was busy securing an eighteen-piece mariachi band. Monteverde was to be at the restaurant at 6:00 P.M. as part of the band, dressed as a mariachi player himself.

There was only one hitch.

The mariachi outfit his father had found for him didn't fit.

Alejandro Gomez Monteverde and Ali Landry at the altar during their wedding in San Miguel, Mexico.

After the wedding all the guests followed a horse-led procession to the reception down the street.

"I found a mariachi that was my size and bought his clothes on the spot," said Monteverde.

All of the other band members were in black. Monteverde's outfit was white. Donning a large sombrero to block his face, Monteverde and the band made their way to the restaurant.

Monteverde's mother excused herself to go to the restroom, leaving Landry alone at the table. As the band approached, Landry thought to herself, "Isn't that nice. The band saw me here alone and is coming to play for me."

Landry never expected that the man in white was Monteverde. She thought he was the lead singer and that he was holding his sombrero to prevent the wind from taking it.

As the mariachi band began playing, Monteverde got down on his knee, doffed the sombrero, handed Landry a ring, and asked her if she would marry him.

"She yelled, 'What are you doing here?' and almost passed out," said Monteverde.

Landry said yes, and the two were married in San Miguel a year later.

On July 10, 2007, as final work was being done on securing a distributor for *Bella*, Alejandro and Ali gave birth to a daughter—Estella Ines. Verástegui agreed to be her godfather.

Leo Severino also found and married his wife Jaquie during the process of making and releasing *Bella*, and they just gave birth to a baby girl named Mina Marie. Sean and Ana Wolfington also had a little baby girl while *Bella* was being made whom they named Isabella—Bella for short.

The Monteverdes, Severinos, and Wolfingtons were not the only ones who had a child as a result of the film. ■

Estella Ines

Isabella "Bella" and Ana Wolfington

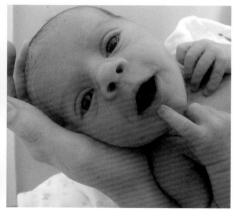
Mina Marie Severino

(Above) The Monteverdes, Wolfingtons, and Severinos all welcomed the birth of baby girls during the *Bella* journey.

(Left) Alejandro Monteverde and wife Ali Landry at their wedding reception in Mexico.

"I never wanted to have children," said Blanchard. "I felt it was pointless." Her attitude changed after making *Bella* and watching the film.

Life
Imitating Art

For Tammy Blanchard, making *Bella* was preparation for real life. After the film had been made but before its release, Blanchard found herself pregnant with her boyfriend Damon Chasmer's child.

"I never wanted to have children," said Blanchard. "I felt it was pointless."

Blanchard's attitude changed after making *Bella* and watching the film.

"Afterwards, I started looking at my body and wondering what it was for," said Blanchard. "I realized that having a child is about producing more love in the world. That's what life is about—love and hope."

She said the film helped give her an appreciation for the entire process of giving life.

"The little girl Sophie [who played Bella] was this little burst of light. She made me realize how special a child is."

Both Blanchard and Chasmer have had a rough life. Chasmer comes from a divorced family, as does Blanchard. She said that coming from such pain helped her to play the broken character of Nina.

"This girl was broke, alone, and living in darkness," explained Blanchard. "She couldn't see any light."

In December 2007, Blanchard and Chasmer gave birth to a baby girl—Ava Jean. ■

New Life
as an Actor

The film also meant "new life" for actor Manny Perez. Perez played the restaurant owner, Manny, in the film.

Prior to *Bella*, Perez, like Verástegui, was relegated to portraying Latino thieves and thugs. Since his role in *Bella*, he said that's changed.

"Being in this film was a true blessing for me," said Perez. "Since *Bella*, I've done fourteen films."

He attributed his success not only to *Bella*, but also to his new appreciation for his faith in God.

Since *Bella*, Perez has done a film with Jennifer Lopez and Marc Anthony, and *Pride and Glory* with Edward Norton and Colin Farrell.

"*Bella* opened a lot of doors for me as an actor," said Perez. "Now, I can be more picky about the roles I take and change the way people look at me. My career can go a different route now.

"On the *Bella* set, there was a feeling that this was about something more powerful than doing a film," added Perez. "When we won the Toronto Film Festival, I felt it was blessed." ■

"I never thought in a million years that by doing my homework I was going to be the instrument that would save this little baby."

First Fruit

Perhaps the most remarkable story is how the film saved the life of an unborn child before it even began production.

Monteverde was in New York trying to find the lead actress; Verástegui was in Los Angeles preparing for the role of a lifetime.

"Because we were working with such a small budget, I knew we had to get it right on the first or second take," said Verástegui. "We didn't have a Nina, but I wanted to understand the pain Nina was going through. I wanted to find a Nina in real life."

Verástegui turned to a friend, Ed Vizenor.

Just three weeks before shooting began on *Bella*, there was still no Nina. Verástegui was getting nervous because he wanted to be prepared for how to handle this very sensitive topic with care and compassion. Vizenor suggested he visit an abortion business to learn more about what women go through.

"I told him that the best way to get to know this character Nina was to understand the women who are going through it."

Vizenor helped Verástegui find an abortion business in Los Angeles. "I did not know what to expect. When I got there, I was shocked to see this line of thirteen- to seventeen-year-old girls," said Verástegui.

Counselors outside the business were trying to speak with the young women. Verástegui introduced himself to the counselors, who mistakenly thought he was one of them. "I wanted to prepare for my role but when I saw all these young girls who were scared and alone I forgot about the movie."

One counselor approached him with a young couple who were scheduled for an abortion but didn't understand English. The couple recognized Verástegui as a celebrity because they were from Mexico where he is very well known.

"I didn't know what I was going to say to them," admitted Verástegui.

"We talked about Mexico, about life, food, our dreams. I shared my life. She shared her life. I told her not to cry, that she wasn't alone, and that I was here to help," said Verástegui. "We talked for nearly an hour."

As a result of talking, the couple missed their appointment for the abortion and had to leave.

"I told them it wasn't a coincidence that we met," said Verástegui. "We exchanged phone numbers, and for the next few days we talked every day."

A few days later, Monteverde hired Tammy Blanchard as the lead actress and Verástegui moved to New York.

"Being there that day, talking with the counselors and that couple, helped me to understand the heart of Nina and other women like her who are scared and alone," said Verástegui. "I was doing *Bella* in real life."

After finishing *Bella*, Verástegui returned to Los Angeles. A few months later, Verástegui received a telephone call from the young man he had met outside the abortion business, the girl's boyfriend.

"He told me that his son had been born the day before, and he wanted to ask my permission to name him Eduardo," said Verástegui. "I put the phone down. I couldn't believe it. It was too much and I started to cry.

"I never thought in a million years that by doing my homework, I was going to be the instrument that would save this little baby," said Verástegui. "If no one ever watched *Bella*, this alone made it worth doing. Eduardito was the first fruit of *Bella*." ■

Bella
Babies

Just as no one could have predicted that Eduardito would be the first fruit, neither could they predict the others that followed.

The second fruit of *Bella* came as the result of a private screening held for influential critics in Miami prior to the movie's release.

At the Miami screening, Eduardo had invited an old friend to come see the movie.

"The guy was like a tornado," said Wolfington. "He came in late and was taking phone calls during the film. He was getting up and leaving, running rampant."

Wolfington worried that the man's behavior might jeopardize the screening. He text-messaged the man asking him to please refrain from taking any more calls during the film. He settled down and watched the movie but did not have the time afterward to share his opinion because he left right when the movie ended.

Three weeks later, Eduardo received a late night telephone call from the man, who told him that a mutual friend of theirs from six years earlier was expecting a child, and that his girlfriend was scheduled to have an abortion at 10:30 A.M. the following morning.

He explained to Eduardo that the mother really wanted to have the baby but that everyone around her was pressuring her to abort her child. The guy told Eduardo that he was the first person he thought of, and asked if Eduardo would call the guy. Eduardo called Wolfington and other friends to ask for advice about what to say. "I was at a loss for words. What can you say to someone in this situation that you have not seen in six years?"

Eduardo felt moved to call the man even though it was 9 P.M. pacific time and midnight in Miami where he lived. "I know about your situation," Verástegui told him. "I'm not here to judge you, but I'm here to let you know that I'm willing to adopt your baby."

Verástegui's offer was met with silence. In the moments that followed, Verástegui wondered whether he was going to be a new father or not.

In the end, they decided to postpone the appointment. Shortly after, Verástegui invited the couple to see the movie along with some important influencers and critics.

"Their faces were red and their eyes were filled with tears," said Wolfington. "At that moment, they were far more important than any critic who was there."

Months after the screening, the couple gave birth to a baby girl, whom they named "Bella." She was the first of many "Bellas."

"Originally, we thought the man that Eduardo had invited was a problem," said Wolfington in retrospect. "Yet, God takes what we perceive as bad circumstances and uses them for great good. It is just a reminder that we often don't see the whole picture and that we need to trust him more than ourselves," said Wolfington.

Sylvia Johnson, executive director of the Houston Pregnancy Help Center, saw the effect of the film firsthand. On November 20, 2007, a particularly busy day at the center, Johnson encountered her first client influenced by the film.

"I very rarely see a client," said Johnson, "but it was a very busy day at the center." On

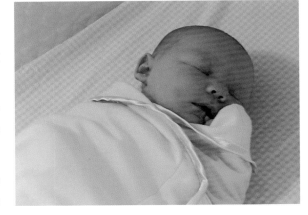

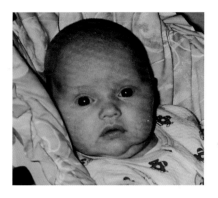

average, the center sees about 240–250 clients per month. "The counselors pulled me, asking if I could counsel a client."

In walked a beautiful, thin, twenty-three-year-old Hispanic woman.

"Originally, the client wanted to abort her child," explained Johnson. "She was single, not married. She told me that she had a younger two-year-old daughter with Down syndrome. As I listened to her, she explained how that had been such a burden on her family. She told me that everyone—her parents and sisters—had to help her with her daughter. She felt she couldn't bring another child into the world and burden her family.

"Then she told me, 'This weekend I saw my favorite Mexican star. I went to see *Bella,*'" recalled Johnson.

Johnson was so struck by the revelation from the tattoo-clad woman that she questioned her.

"You saw *Bella*? You saw that movie?" asked Johnson.

The young woman said that she had told Johnson that she didn't think she could have the abortion.

"I didn't have to do any counseling," said Johnson. "The movie did it for me."

According to Johnson, the young woman was grateful for seeing the film.

"The movie impacted her so much," said Johnson. "She had changed her decision the Saturday after seeing the film."

That story was repeated across the country.

After word got out about *Bella*'s impact on mothers who were facing unexpected pregnancies, counselors from across the country saw the movie as a non-judgmental way to help young women see beyond their fear so they could make the choice that was best for them and their child.

On Saturday, December 1, 2007, John Stewart was counseling outside the Memphis Center for Reproductive Health, an abortion business in Memphis, Tennessee.

On this particular Saturday morning, Stewart spoke with a Hispanic couple in their twenties from northern Mississippi. The young woman had lived for a time in California and knew English. The young man knew little English.

"During the course of their conversation, Stewart asked the woman if she had heard of the movie *Bella.*

"I asked her if she wanted to see the movie before making a final decision," said Stewart. "She said she would."

The woman cancelled her appointment to abort her child and instead went to see *Bella* in the theater. The couple decided to attend a showing at a Bartlett, Tennessee, theater they were familiar with. Having some time before the showing, Stewart invited them to a nearby Chinese restaurant for lunch. "They seemed very much in love," said Stewart.

After lunch, the three attended a showing at a Malco Theater in Bartlett. "I sensed during the movie that she was moved," said Stewart.

After walking outside to the parking lot, they visited briefly. Stewart gave the couple his telephone number and recommended that they get in touch with a local Care Net pregnancy center for assistance.

"She said the movie made a difference," said Stewart. "The film provided the encouragement that she needed to continue with her pregnancy."

Tracy Reynolds, media liaison with the San Antonio-based Justice Foundation and its international project Operation Outcry, knows of three other cases of mothers who chose adoption over abortion because of seeing *Bella*.

"We work with pregnancy care centers around the country," said Reynolds. "We are aware of women in New Hampshire, Florida, and California who were pregnant, and the film helped give them hope."

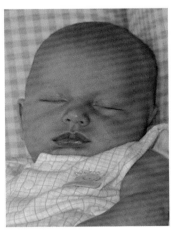

Reynolds, who does some volunteer work at a local pregnancy care center, said she personally spoke with a Hispanic waitress in Roseville, California, who went ahead with her pregnancy because of the impact of the film.

"She had gone to see the movie as a matter of course because it was a Latino film," said Reynolds. "She said that before the film, she and her boyfriend were uncertain what to do, but the film absolutely convinced them that they needed to keep and raise the baby."

Another woman Reynolds heard about was then-twenty-year-old Leigha Leary of New Hampshire.

A college junior, Leary first discovered she was pregnant in June of 2007. It wasn't part of her immediate future plans.

"I was caught pretty off-guard," said Leary. "I had my life plans made. I was majoring in

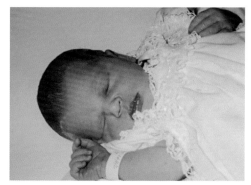

communications and hoped to open a day spa. I was pretty upset when I found out."

Leary's boyfriend, Ramsey Lawrence, was caught by surprise, too. The two had met at college and shared communication classes.

"I never wanted to have an abortion, but it seemed easier," said Leary.

So Leary scheduled an initial appointment at an abortion business. Lawrence went with her. "We talked to a woman about the options—adoption, abortion, keeping the baby," said Leary. "I was so indecisive."

Lawrence reached out to a woman he knew through church, Kelly Roy, who had been through an abortion seven years earlier. "I got a phone call late one night from Ramsey telling me that his girlfriend was pregnant and scared," said Roy.

Roy herself had become pregnant and given birth to a daughter while a high school senior. While in college, she became pregnant again and sought an abortion. The abortion business botched the abortion. Two days later, Roy passed the baby girl at home.

"I could see her eyes, her hands, her feet," said Roy. "I went into shock, lost tons of weight, and dropped out of college."

Through the help of her parents and counseling, Roy was able to go through recovery and healing. "I talked to Leary and shared my story with her," said Roy. "I told her what happened and shared the pain and grief I went through, and told her I didn't want her to go through it. I just tried to be there for her and call her when she was scared."

"She would call when I was breaking down," recalled Leary. "We would pray together and she would pray for me."

Leary received tremendous support from Roy, and from her boyfriend Ramsey and his parents. Leigha and Ramsey frequently went on long walks on the beach to discuss their options.

When *Bella* opened in theaters in New Hampshire, Roy made it to one of the first showings. "I went with some other people," said Roy. "The theater was so crowded they had to put it in a larger theater."

When she exited the theater, there standing in front of her, waiting to go in, was Leigha, Ramsey, and his parents.

Roy told Leary: "You're going to bawl. You're going to love it. It's such a special movie."

Leary said she loved it.

"The movie had parts that made me laugh—such as the encounter with the parents—and parts that made me cry, which helped me relate to the challenge that I was going through," she said.

Leary found that she could really identify with the characters. It was like watching a movie of their life.

"The movie struck close to home," said Leary. "With their walks on the beach it reminded me a lot of us. I was like Nina—shocked. Ramsey was like José—so supportive and really strong. The movie was healing and therapeutic."

Within the weeks following the film, Leary decided to name the child Isabella if the baby was a girl.

"We didn't know if it would be a girl or boy," said Leary. "But I believed deep in my heart that it was a girl and we would name her Isabella."

Leigha and Ramsey were married on a wintery snowy evening, December 14, 2008. On March 29, 2008, baby Isabella Grace was born to the couple. They call her Bella for short.

"The whole thing was so amazing how it all worked out," said Roy.

Crisis pregnancy centers found the film a useful tool in their work. So much so that the film has taken on new life since its May 2008 DVD release.

While the film was in theaters, Reynolds encouraged clients who were on the fence to go see the movie. She said that pregnancy counseling centers have been purchasing the DVD for use in counseling.

"It's a natural tool," said Reynolds. "The story is real and poignant, but not heavy-handed."

It is hard for people to see clearly in the midst of a crisis pregnancy. When they are filled with fear, it often leads them to feel like they have no choice at all. Watching a real world story they can relate to helps them rise above their fears. They see there is a bigger picture, and most of all they see that there is hope.

Anne Lotierzo, executive director of the Fort Pierce, Florida-based Pregnancy Care Center, said that she saw the impact of the film at their crisis pregnancy center immediately after the DVD became available. The first evening Lotierzo had the DVD, she played it in the center's waiting room. That night three teenagers came into the center, two girls and a boy.

"Both of the girls wanted to take pregnancy tests," said Lotierzo. "By the time I had finished seeing one, the other girl had gotten through a good part of the movie. As I walked her back to

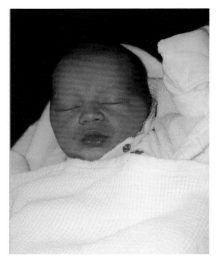

the counseling room, I casually asked her what she thought of the film.

"She said, 'Now I know I'm not alone,'" said Lotierzo. "It impacted me and brought back the fears and the loneliness that young teens feel when they come in for a pregnancy test. We see the same scenario over and over, but for each of them it's like they have blinders on. They only see what's in front of them."

The film offered them the opportunity to address the fears and worries that she had—fears about her parents, about her boyfriend's parents, about returning to school pregnant in the fall.

"I felt the film was the key to opening the door to the session," said Lotierzo.

The film's unforeseen ability to positively affect women caught in crisis pregnancies has led pregnancy center leaders to describe the film as an "entertainment ultrasound," referring to the significant impact that an ultrasound often has in helping a mother see the value of her unborn child.

Tracy Reynolds said, "The difference with the movie is that with ultrasound, you still have the fear of how you're going to cope. *Bella* goes beyond by giving you hope."

Recognizing the film's potential in this regard, Jason Jones created the Hero Foundation (Human Rights Education and Relief Organization) and the "Great Campaign for Human Dignity." As part of that campaign, Jones is raising $3 million to provide a copy of *Bella* to any pregnant woman who requests one.

Jones, who serves on the board of the Pearson Centers, is working with Care Net and Heartbeat International's network of eighteen hundred affiliated crisis pregnancy centers to make the film available. In addition, Jones set up a website called www.BellaHeroes.com, where the organization is accepting donations for covering the costs of supplying DVDs to crisis pregnancy centers that need them.

Another group that has been greatly affected by the film is people who have had abortions in the past. Tracy Reynolds is one of those.

Reynolds first saw the film at a Texas screening with Governor Rick Perry. The Justice Foundation became one of hundreds of organizations that helped support and promote the film.

In September 2007, Reynolds saw the film a second time, at a Care Net conference in Kentucky.

"The first time I saw it, I loved it," said Reynolds. "The second time I saw it, it touched my heart on a personal level."

The next evening, Reynolds dreamed about the little girl whom she had aborted years earlier.

"I cried through many states on the drive home," admitted Reynolds. "I came to the conclusion that I wanted to do whatever I could to support *Bella* and to be more active in crisis pregnancy center work."

While the film was in theaters, Reynolds passed out fliers on the movie to clients. Since its DVD release, she's purchased twenty copies to distribute to pregnancy centers and clients.

She isn't alone.

The film has inspired other women to become more active in pregnancy counseling as well.

"Women who have experienced abortions wish that they had a José in their lives," said Reynolds. "They're promoting the film in their communities."

"Many of us began praying regularly for the movie and Metanoia for protection and success," said Lisa Dudley, director of outreach for Operation Outcry. "The weekend it opened in San Antonio was the same weekend as our annual retreat. I took all the ladies to see the movie. Tears ran and hearts were moved.

"I don't know anyone in Operation Outcry who was not impacted and committed to help this movie," said Dudley. "As God continued to have our paths cross, the *Bella* team named us *Bella*'s Angels."

Bella's Angels presented actor Verástegui with a special sculpture, called The Hope Monument. Based on a larger sculpture, the statue depicts a woman holding the hand of Jesus.

"For us, the statue reminded us of José holding the hand of Nina," said Reynolds.

"Many of these women who have seen *Bella* have said, 'If only I would have had a José in my life, I wouldn't have aborted my child,'" said Reynolds. "Many have purchased advance copies of the DVD and want to use them to help others in similar situations." ■

A Trend?

The makers of *Bella* couldn't have predicted that other films dealing with teen pregnancy would open in the same year, but it happened. In the months prior to *Bella*, *Knocked Up* opened, as did *Waitress*. In the months following *Bella*, *August Rush* and *Juno* opened.

As a result of the popularity of the films, the National Council for Adoption launched a public service advertising campaign in March 2008. The council utilized television, radio, and billboards to spread the message that, "Sometimes choosing adoption is being a good mother."

"We see the movies as an opportunity to promote adoption awareness," Thomas Atwood, president of the National Council for Adoption told *USA Today*. "Infant adoption is ripe for growth, for revival."

Hollywood insiders can't say whether the films represent a growing trend, but do say they're worth taking note.

"The public goes to see movies with faith and values," said Ted Baehr, founder and publisher of *Movieguide*. "Three of the five had positive Christian values. I think this will be a growing number of films."

Not all were happy with the string of pro-life themed films.

It appears some critics were annoyed that none of the pregnant characters in these films chose to abort their children. "I think it's shocking that the subject of abortion as a choice has been so eliminated from the discussion," Jennifer Merin, president of the Alliance of Women Film Journalists told the *Washington Post*. "It's not even on the table."

Washington Post writer Ann Hornaday described *Waitress* and *Knocked Up* as flawed. "Both films are predicated on unplanned pregnancies and both confect, through all manner of narrative conceits and messy logic, reasons for their female protagonists to carry their unwanted babies to term," wrote Hornaday.

Culture and Media Institute's senior writer Kristen Fyfe responded to the criticism by saying that "Hornaday can't fathom a world—the real world—where some people, regardless of marital status, will choose to carry a pregnancy to term. Will choose to give birth to the human being growing within them. Will choose life," wrote Fyfe. ▪

Living Oscars

While the film-makers had hoped that their movie might garner Oscar attention, as other Toronto International Film Festival People's Choice Award winners had, they aren't disappointed. The film was one of the most honored films of the year, and they are most happy with the other "awards" they've received.

As this book goes to press, the filmmakers were aware of at least fifteen *Bella* babies—children who exist as a result of their mothers who decided not to abort their children after seeing the movie.

"I don't take a single dust of credit," said Monteverde. "I know it wasn't me or anyone else in the team. I'm amazed, and it gives me encouragement to keep making films like this."

"The living Oscars have been the babies saved and the babies adopted," said Severino. "I'm just happy the Lord let us be part of it."

Appendixes

Impact on the Youth

The *Bella* team conducted an essay contest with students from grade schools, high schools and some college students. Below you will find some of the thoughts from various students ranging in age from ten years old to twenty-one years old. It is beautiful to read their thoughts about the movie and how it impacted their lives. It is also surprising how they all seemed to capture the same essence despite their different ages.

Grade Schoolers

Let's begin by reading the impressions from the grade schoolers. While most do not include the student's name all of these kids are ten to fourteen years old.

My name is Jerry Orlando and I'm an eighth grade student from St. Monica School. On November 2nd I went to see the movie *Bella* and it was just what the title means, beautiful. It is a great movie for people of age 13 and up. *Bella* puts forth a great message. You are responsible for all your actions even if you later regret them. The movie also shows the importance of family and friends, how you can always count on your family for help, no matter how bad the situation is. I think all teenagers should see this movie to teach them a lesson about life. I also believe that this movie will help answer their questions about life and teach them to think twice about rushing too fast into a relationship with someone they don't really have feelings for. *Bella* will bring a tear to your eye. It will also keep you glued to the screen waiting to see what will happen next. This is not a movie that I will praise and then forget about. It has been a life lesson I will not soon forget. After viewing this movie you will want to recommend it to everyone you talk to. If I ever have a question about something I did or about life itself I will remember this movie.

＝

This movie helps you appreciate life better and respect other people. This is the kind of a movie you go to see over and over and never get tired of it. After seeing this movie, I have a whole new view on life. The movie got me thinking of my own life and had me asking questions like, Do I take responsibility for my actions? Am I there for my family and friends when they need me? Do I appreciate life? and finally, Am I happy with myself? I've learned from this movie that in order to love others, you have to love yourself. If you do not take the time from your schedule to go see a one of a kind movie, you are passing up a chance of a lifetime.

＝

The movie *Bella* is an incredible movie with an even more incredible message. For me, this message was one of God's incredible plan and how the bad things in our lives can help us change. All of this boils down to trust in God. We trust that God created all of us for a special purpose. We trust that everything happens for a reason and that God can turn everything around. When we trust in God, all things will fall into place. We need to remember that everyone is here because God wanted them to be, therefore we should treat each other with respect and love. We also need to be more positive about everything. Not every bad thing that happens is the end of the world, in fact it's probably just a way for God to strengthen and bring us together. *Bella* was a powerful movie about life, love, and God that really helped me with my faith and I'm thankful I had the opportunity to see it.

＝

You can see God working through both José and Nina as they help each other open up, trust and start over. I think this movie is wonderful because it shows how anyone's life can change at any moment.

＝

I was deeply moved at the humanity represented by each character and circumstance despite the demoralized world we live in today. *Bella* embraces genuineness. For those 90 minutes I truly appreciated the beauty in the world.

Winning Grade School Essay

This is an excerpt from the winner of the essay contest

My father once told me a story that made me think and now I understand what he was talking about. Once there was a man, who asked God for a flower and a butterfly but instead God gave him a cactus and a caterpillar. The man was sad. He did not understand why his request was mistaken then he thought, oh well, God has too many people to care for and decided not to question his action. After some time he went to check on his cactus that he had forgotten about. To his surprise, from the thorny ugly cactus, a beautiful flower had grown. The unsightly caterpillar had been transformed in to the most beautiful butterfly. What you want is not always what you need. God always does things right. His way is always the best way, even if to us it seems all wrong. If anyone asks God for one thing and receives another, trust him. You can be sure that he will always give you what you need at the appropriate time. This was evident to Nina and José. God gives the very best to those who leave the choices to him.

High School and College Students

Now let's read the impressions of the high school and college students who range in age from fifteen years old to twenty-one years old.

B*ella* is a movie that has the power to change many lives. The underlying themes of love and life throughout the movie are amazing. In today's culture, we need more films like *Bella* to show the young generation that they're loved, how to love and respect others. Many people today grow up in households where they do not experience love because of divorce, violence or something as simple as incredibly busy schedules. We need to reach out to this generation before it's too late and let them know what love is and that they are loved. The *Bella* movie is a wonderful way to bring love into the home. The love shown in the movie is a wonderful model for young people in today's society. In the media today, young people are being told that sex is love and if you love your boyfriend or girlfriend you should have sex. However, *Bella* shows us that love is not based on a sexual relationship, but rather it should come out of friendship and total acceptance of another person. This is the type of love that we should be showing young people today. It kept me motivated to pray for all those who are in a difficult situation and do not know what to do. Just one person's prayer can change the life of another, forever. It also shows how the love of one person, even if they're just an acquaintance, can change someone's life. I am now more aware.

≈

Nobody can go back and start a new beginning, but anyone can start today and make a new ending. The critically acclaimed movie *Bella* tells a tale about life appreciation and creating a new ending. Life is full of mistakes and tragedy, the best way to overcome that is to live and move forward. *Bella* showed that life is precious and worth living. Life is valuable. There are moments when every person feels that he or she cannot move forward, but you can start today.

≈

Bella serves as a radiant beacon of hope for our troubled world. The movie portrays the importance of family, friendship, relationships, choices, forgiveness, and especially love. This movie is not a love story between two people but it is a story about love and understanding of all people. *Bella* captures humanity in a compassionate and uplifting way.

≈

The first words in *Bella* were, "If you want to make God laugh tell him your plans." This single line summarizes the key message from *Bella*. It explains that though we may plan out our future, we are first called to seek the will of God. *Bella*'s symbolism subtly directs the audience to look to God and reach out for guidance.

≈

If we open our eyes to God and let him into our life, we will have a deeper relationship with Christ. Such as that of the blind beggar in *Bella*. In this movie especially, God is revealed through the lowly, desolate, and suppressed. The beggar and José in particular were able to help others in their life by their own trials and tribulations. By Nina having the child, José is able to adopt the girl and bring back the passion he lost after the accident. I learned from this movie that no matter how bad the situation or dilemma you are in, with God's help and guidance you can find hope.

≈

I believe that it is very appropriate that this movie was produced by Metonoia Productions because hopefully many people will experience a metanoia in their heart as a result of seeing *Bella*.

≈

So here we have the thoughts of young people from thirteen to age twenty-one with completely different levels of writing skills, but they all seem to grasp the same message. The more I read their thoughts the more impressed I am with their depth and wisdom at such a young age. I think we can all benefit from seeing the world from their perspective every once in a while.

Winning High School Essay

These are excerpts from the winner of the essay contest

It has been a long time since a love story like *Bella* has touched my heart so profoundly. I originally believed that this movie was going to be about the struggles of abortion and end up being a sappy love story. I was surprised to learn that this movie was a different kind of love story, a story about the love of a family.

"Bella" is Italian for "beautiful." Beautiful is English for something extraordinary or incredible. What is more beautiful than the unconditional love of a family? José knows that his family will always be there for him, no matter what circumstances occur. But what about someone with no family for support? In my opinion, family is not determined by blood, but by those special people who stand by you no matter what, who help you in any time of need, the ones who love you unconditionally. Although Nina does not realize it at first, José is her family. José does not judge Nina, he does not tell her what to do, he does not walk away when they disagree; he listens to her, he allows her to be herself, but most importantly he loves her. This movie touched me personally because the intense love that José's family has for their son is so great that he is able to pass it on to someone else. My family has always been very loving to me and has always taught me that family doesn't stop with genetics. When you pass on a little love, when you share a little "family," it can mean the world to someone.

Many would perceive this movie as I first did, but when you take a closer look at its true message, it has tremendous potential for all kinds of interpretation. The world can seem to be a confusing and lonely place, especially today with all the wars and hate circulating around the globe. Fortunately this movie portrays the importance of acceptance in all forms. *Bella* shows how you must not only accept others (as José and his family accepted Nina for who she was), but how you must accept yourself. Nina had the feeling that it was her against the world, like everyone was out to get her. She really never gave herself a chance to open up to the joys that surrounded her. Her journey with José to see his family really helped her realize that the first step to loving others is to love yourself.

This movie could be interpreted in many ways, but the ways I have mentioned are how *Bella* touched me personally, and how I believe that it can affect our world today. This little girl Bella symbolizes second chances, new life, and hope.

Winning College Essay

American movie culture requires that directors and actors adopt a full disclosure approach to films. However, in light of society's daunting tendencies toward violence, sexual assault, pornography, and adultery, would it not be prudent to incorporate a modest, less-is-more method? The poignant and beautifully crafted film *Bella* embodies such an intricately woven work of art void of crude sex scenes, incessant bloodshed and vulgar language. Yet, *Bella* still manages to convey an inspiring message of love and family and how their presence or absence in a person's life fundamentally affects human choice.

José and Nina are not merely stock characters, and their profound love proceeds from sincere human intimacy, not superficial physical interaction. They represent real people who wrestle with inner demons yet manage to possess compassion; neither character is clearly black or white in disposition. *Bella* delves deep into the heart of a person and challenges us to recognize our shortcomings in order to love our whole selves unconditionally, just as God does. José carries his accident with him and refuses to believe it was merely an accident until he has the opportunity to rectify his mistake by showing Nina the value of life. Nina, although not haunted by the past, refuses to accept her impending future and through encountering the love of a true family she struggles with her selfish outlook on the sanctity of life.

Each symbolic transition from past to present to future examines the characters and their growth not as trivial specks in the grand scheme of the universe but rather as involved participants in God's design. The blind man, although unnoticed in a chaotic city such as New York, desires to know the simplest details of life because just as the film employs a less is more form, the content reveals the significance of individuals and their impact on one another.

Life cannot be measured by the amount of money we make or the number of people who we control; the measure of life relies on our experience and the people who are with us along the way. *Bella* recognizes the superficiality of José's lucrative soccer career and Manny's posh restaurant in order to identity the blinding effect of materialism. The symbolism forces society to peer past the facades of culture and value the purity in all God's creation.

I was deeply moved at the humanity represented by each character and circumstance because despite the demoralized world we live in today, *Bella* embraces genuineness and for those ninety minutes I truly appreciated the beauty in the world.

Timeline

February 2004	Alejandro arrives in Los Angeles from Austin, Texas, with the story of *Bella* in his head from the drive.
March 2004	Eduardo and Leo meet at Mass at Good Shepherd Catholic Church Palm Sunday; the following Monday, Metanoia Films is formed.
May–July 2004	Alejandro goes off to the mountains to write first draft of *Bella*.
August–November 2004	Leo joins Alejandro in isolation to help finish the script.
November 2004	Three Amigos go completely broke and are about to call it quits.
November 2004	Eduardo is blessed by Pope John Paul the Great.
December 2004	Metanoia meets Sean and Eustace Wolfington who fund the project and company without seeing the script.
May 2005	Pre-production of *Bella* begins in New York.
June 2005	Eduardo researching his role goes to first abortion clinic; nine months later little Eduardo is born.
July 2005	Leo and Eduardo move in with the Franciscan Friars of the Renewal in Washington Heights.
August 15, 2005	*Bella* principal photography begins for twenty-four days.
September 15, 2005	Rain miracle on set.
Early October 2005	First assembly of *Bella* is finished.
December 2005	First cut of *Bella* finished.
December 8, 2005	First public screening of *Bella* with focus groups; *Bella* scores through the roof!
January–May 2006	Post production of *Bella* continues; grass-roots tour with early cuts of *Bella* begins.

Late March 2006	First final cut of *Bella*; first *Bella* film print.
Summer 2006	Grass-roots efforts continue; acceptance in Toronto Film Festival.
September 7, 2006	First screening of *Bella* at Toronto.
September 16, 2006	*Bella* wins Toronto.
Fall 2006	Screening in Miami that will result nine months later in the birth of Bella (little girl saved from abortion).
2007	Grass-roots efforts continue until film release.
April 2007	Meet Pope Benedict with first cut of *Bella* on DVD for his blessing.
October 26, 2007	*Bella* released in U.S. theaters.
April 11, 2008	*Bella* opens internationally in Mexico, Canada, Australia, and New Zealand.
May 6, 2008	*Bella* released on DVD and Eduardo appears on *The Today Show* with Kathie Lee Gifford.
May 6–May 28, 2008	*Bella* remains the #1 Top selling DVD on Amazon in its category (love and romance). *Bella* is the #6 top rated movie of all time on Yahoo.com, one of the largest websites in the world.
September 2008	The *Behind Bella* book and the *Bella* soundtrack are released.

Reviews

"Warm, sweet and funny."
Roger Ebert, RogerEbert.com

"One of the best films I've seen in a long time."
Maria Salas, NBC-Miami

"The Best movie of the Year. Everyone should see this film."
Rick Warren, *The Purpose Driven Life*

"A Perfect Film, An Artistic Masterpiece."
Tony Bennett, Grammy & Emmy Award Winning Singer/Songwriter

"A sweet, life-affirming picture"
Gary Goldstein, *Los Angeles Times*

"A bear-hugging embrace of sweetness and light"
Stephen Holden, *New York Times*

"Cynics need not apply, but I found *Bella* a real heart tugger."
Lou Lumenick, *New York Post*

"An unforgettable experience! A celebration of family, food, music and life-affirming values."
Michael Medved

"Versatégui is a natural on the big screen, a compelling presence."
Ruthe Stein, *San Francisco Chronicle*

"Powerful and moving . . . a true inspiration."
CNN, Ana Maria Montero

"The warmest family drama I've seen in years."
Frank Lovece, *Film Journal*

"*Bella* is an irrefutably effortless and heartwarming film, an indie gem with a deep soul and a beautiful message."
Brandon Fibbs, *Colorado Springs Gazette*

"A beautiful film [with] pitch-perfect performances. A film that embraces and celebrates the possibility for change and growth, both personal and spiritual."
   Austin Chronicle

"Not only will *Bella* give you hope that Hollywood can still make an inspirational movie, it might also renew your faith in humanity."
   Governor Rick Perry, Texas

"Watching *Bella* is a miracle that will touch your heart and transform your soul."
   Ted Baehr, *Movieguide*

"*Bella* is a moving and inspirational movie. In a day of Hollywood's excesses, profanities, and foolishness, this sensitive film speaks eloquently of life, love, and beauty."
   Dr. James Dobson, Founder of Focus on the Family

"It is a powerful movie that reveals the beauty of sacrificial love."
   Jim Daly, President of Focus on the Family

"*Bella* masterfully and powerfully captures the best things of life: family, the value of unborn life, unconditional love and redemption. *Bella* is a 10! You must see this movie!"
   Dr. Dennis Rainey, President of Family Life

"This is a powerful, uplifting, stirring story that will be talked about for a long, long time. This is the kind of movie you can feel free to take anybody to and people are going to have unbelievable discussions afterwards. It's got a very subtle plot too that turns in a way that takes your breath away."
   Bill Hybels, Willow Creek

"*Bella* is the kind of movie that the public would love to see come out of Hollywood more often... it will inspire you and warm your heart."
   Rush Limbaugh

Resources

Adoption

National Council for Adoption

NCFA has been a champion of adoption since its founding in 1980. Whether as an advocate for state laws that promote sound adoption policy, a resource for federal officials and policymakers about appropriate federal adoption initiatives and reform, a diplomat for sound international adoption policy, or a source of adoption facts and education, NCFA is devoted to serving the best interests of children through adoption. Learn more about the ways in which NCFA works to promote the positive option of adoption.

 1-703-299-6633 www.adoptioncouncil.org

Bethany Christian Services

 Headquartered in Grand Rapids, Michigan, Bethany is a not-for-profit, pro-life, Christian adoption and family services agency.

 1-800-BETHANY www.bethany.org

Crisis Pregnancy

Option Line

 Care Net provides information on abortion alternatives, free pregnancy tests, and adoption; connects you with local centers for free counseling; provides mapping to local centers.

 1-800-395-HELP (1-800-395-4357) www.care-net.org

Heartbeat International

 www.heartbeatinternational.org

Prolife Across America

 1-800-366-7773 www.prolifeacrossamerica.com

Prenatal Partners for Life

 Website contains both information and testimonies of parents who have faced the diagnosis of a serious birth defect such as trisomy 18 or Down syndrome. It offers the chance for parents to contact those whose stories appear for more support.

 1-763-772-3868 www.prenatalpartnersforlife.org

Her Choice

You can listen to recordings made by people who have faced the abortion question. These are real life abortion-related testimonies made by people who were in situations similar to what you may be in now. They will tell you about the pressures they were under, the paths they chose, and the results of their choice.

1-952-223-1374   www.herchoice.org

National Life Center

National Life Center is the parent corporation to the 1st Way Pregnancy Centers across the country. They are able to network and directly connect to over 3,500 centers throughout the U.S.

1-800-848 (LOVE) 5683   www.nationallifecenter.com

Post-Abortion Recovery

The National Office of Post-Abortion Reconciliation and Healing

The National Office of Post-Abortion Reconciliation and Healing, Inc. networks researchers and psychotherapeutic professionals working in the field within the U.S. and abroad, consults on the formation of post-abortion support services within secular and religious settings.

1-800-5WE-CARE   www.noparh.org

Abortion Recovery Helpline

1-866-482-LIFE

Operation Outcry

www.operationoutcry.org

Project Rachel

Project Rachel is a healing ministry of the Catholic Church for those who have been involved in abortion.

1-888-329-3773   www.hopeafterabortion.com

Rachel's Vineyard

Rachel's Vineyard is a safe place to renew, rebuild, and redeem hearts broken by abortion. Weekend retreats offer you a supportive, confidential, and non-judgmental environment where women and men can express, release, and reconcile painful post-abortive emotions to begin the process of restoration, renewal, and healing.

1-877-467-3463   www.rachelsvineyard.org

Silent No More

An effort to make the public aware of the devastation abortion brings to women, men, and their families.

www.silentnomoreawareness.org

Cast and Crew

Actor	Character
Eduardo Verástegui	José
Tammy Blanchard	Nina
Manny Perez	Manny
Ali Landry	Celia
Angelica Aragon	Mother
Jaime Tirelli	Father
Ramon Rodriguez	Eduardo
Lukas Behnken	Johannes
Peter Bucossi	Angry Driver
David Castro	Boy #1
Michael Chin	Bodega Clerk
Dominic Colón	Pepito
Hudson Cooper	Husband
Tawny Cypress	Frannie
Ewa Da Cruz	Veronica
Sara Dawson	Helen
Doug DeBeech	Pieter
Alexa Gerasimovich	Loochi
Anthony Ippolito	Boy on Subway
Herb Lovelle	Homeless Man
Matlock	Teen performer
Michael Mosley	Kevin
Wade Mylius	J.J.
Stan Newman	Businessman on Phone
Sophie Nyweide	Bella
Kola Ogundiran	Cabbie
Melinda Peinado	Nurse
Alfonso Ramirez	Leonardo
Armando Riesco	Francisco
Jamie Schofield	Hostess
James Stanek	Henri
Marilyn Torres	Carla
Ana Baena Wolfington	Woman at Turnstyle
Teresa Yenque	Amelia

Drumatics:

Subway Drummers	William Johnson, Maurice Carr, Yuichi Iida

Director: Alejandro Gomez Monteverde

Screenwriters: Alejandro Gomez Monteverde, Patrick Million, Leo Severino

Producers: Alejandro Monteverde, Leo Severino, Eduardo Verástegui, Denise Pinckley, and Sean Wolfington

Executive Producers: J. Eustace Wolfington, Sean Wolfington, Marcy Wolfington, Ana Wolfington, and Steve McEveety

Co-Executive Producers: Mark Follett, Bob Atwell, David Hackney, J.S. Jones, John Shepherd, Fred Foote, Ken Foote

Associate Producers: Dan Genetti, Glen Trotiner, Matthew Malek, Ryan Wolfington

Director of Photography: Andrew Cadelago

Editors: Fernando Villena, Joseph Gutowski

Music: Stephan Altman

Production Design: Richard Lassalle

Costume Designer: Eden Miller

Music Supervisor: Frankie Pine

Special Thanks

Adam DeGraide
Adrienne Hynek
Alan Chambers
Alan Sears
Alejandro Herrera
Alejandro Ramirez
Alejandro Sanz
Alex Wolfington
Alexis Walkenstein
Alfonso Aguilar
Alfonso Montiel
Alicia San Pedro de Cordoba
Allen Arnold
Amalia Zea-Meadows
Amanda Fox
Amanda Melefsky
Amber Larkin
Amelia Estrada
Ami McConnell
Amy Herman
Andrew Smith
Andrew Walther
Andy Fraser
Angela Baraquio Grey
Angela King
Anita Crane
Ann Bierschenk
Ann Corkery
Ann Hubbel
Annie Kate Pons
Anthony J. Ryan
Antonio Berumen
April Krieger
April Salazar
Araceli Marquez
Archbishop Alfred C. Hughes
Archbishop Daniel N. Dinardo
Archbishop Daniel Pilarcyzk
Archbishop George H. Niederauer
Archbishop Oscar H. Lipscomb
Archbishop Raymond Burke
Archbishop Wilton D. Gregory
Armando Correa
Arturo Chavez
Arturo Garcia
Barbara Hester
Barbara Nicolosi

Becky Norton Dunlop
Beverlee Dean
Beverly Kastens
Bill Hybels
Bird Matson
Bishop Bernard J. Harrington
Bishop Carl Mengeling
Bishop Clarence Silva
Bishop David Zubik
Bishop Dennis M. Schnurr
Bishop Edward James Slattery
Bishop Edward P. Cullen
Bishop Frederick Campbell
Bishop George Leo Thomas
Bishop George W. Coleman
Bishop Gerald F. Kicanas
Bishop Gerald M. Barbarito
Bishop Glen Provost
Bishop Greg Aymond
Bishop James A. Tamayo
Bishop James E. Kurtz
Bishop John D'Arcy
Bishop John F. Kinney
Bishop John M. Smith
Bishop Joseph Adamec
Bishop Kevin C. Rhoades
Bishop Kevin Farrell
Bishop Leonard Blair
Bishop Martin Amos
Bishop Michael Burbidge
Bishop Michael Jackels
Bishop Michael Jarrell
Bishop Paul A. Zipfel
Bishop Paul Bootkowski
Bishop Paul S. Coakley
Bishop Randolph R. Calvo
Bishop Ricardo Ramirez
Bishop Richard Malone
Bishop Robert Meunch
Bishop Robert Morlino
Bishop Robert Vasa
Bishop Roger Foys
Bishop Salvatore Cordileone
Bishop Sam Jacobs
Bishop Samuel Aquila
Bishop Thomas Rodi
Bob Angelotti

Br. Agustino Torres
Bradley Robertson
Brian J. Conaty
Brian O'Neil
Brian Trainor
Briana Guzman
Bridget Hackney
Britni Karst
Brooke Burns
Bryan Kemper
Cardinal Daniel DiNardo
Cardinal Justine Rigali
Cardinal of Mexico
Cardinal Sean O'Malley
Carl Anderson
Carlos & Dorothy Alfonso
Carlos Garcia
Carlos Villalobos
Carolyn Paul
Cassidy Gifford
Cathy Chermol
Cathy Crukavina
Cathy Kilingman
Cecelia Price
Cecile Martin-Houlgatte
Cheryl Nagakubo
Chris & Marie Smith
Chris Aubert
Chris Donahue
Chris LaChance
Chris Slattery
Christian Kaplan
Christina Valentine
Christine Bae
Christine Codden
Christopher A. Wills
Christopher West
Cindy Black
Clare Ruehl
Cody Gifford
Cody Griffith
Colin Wickstrom
Conchita Paz-Oliva
Congressman Chris Smith & wife
    Marie Smith
Coni Gerhart
Cris Fischer

D. James Kennedy
Dale J. Melczek
Dale Noble
Damon Kidwell & 71 Design Team
Dan Andriacco & Carl Brown
Daniel Conlon
Daniel Garza
Daniel Heneghan
Daniella Lopez
David Colletti
David Hannah
David Kiersznowski
David Ricken
Daymond Decker
Deacon David Montgomery
Deacon Mike Chiappetta
Deal Hudson
Deanne Ward
Deby Schlapprizzi
Deirdre McQuade
Denis & Cathy Nolan
Dennis Rainey
Derry & Lidy Connelly
Diana Diaz
Dick Bott
Dino Vlahakis
Dirt Poor Robbins
Don Francisco
Donald Wildmon
Dorene Dominguez
Doug Brown
Drew Marioni
Ed Vizenor
Edgar "Shoboy" Sotelo
Eduardo Garcia Jimenez
Edward Tsai
El Gordo Cadelago
Elena Dilion
Elena Fiske
Elizabeth Disco-Shearer
Elizabeth Ferguson
Elizabeth Graham
Emilio Larroza
Emilio Moure
Emily Christianson
Eric Day
Eric Genuis

Erica Tarin
Erick Bell
Erik Lokesome
Erin Hanson
Erin McCrory
Ernesto Peralta
Erwin McManus
Esperanza Griffith
Estafano
Esther Fleece
Eugenio Cobo
Fr. Daniel Massick, L.C.
Fr. Don Woznicki
Fr. Emilio Diaz, L.C.
Fr. Eric Hastings
Fr. Francisco Alanis
Fr. Frank Pavone
Fr. Jeffrey Bowlker
Fr. Jerome Molokie, O.Praem.
Fr. John Bartunek
Fr. John Cihak
Fr. John Connor, L.C.
Fr. John Donahue, L.C.
Fr. John Janze
Fr. John Morris
Fr. Jonathan Meyer
Fr. Joseph Fessio, S.J.
Fr. Juan Guerra, L.C.
Fr. Juan Rivas, L.C.
Fr. Justin Sergio Ramos, O.Praem.
Fr. Leo Joseph Fisher, C.F.R.
Fr. Luke Mary Fletcher, C.F.R.
Fr. Theodore Mennes
Fr. Thomas Euteneuer
Fr. Vincent Gil, L.C.
Fr. Willy Raymond
Family Theater Productions
Federico Muñoz
Fernan Martinez
Filomeno Martinez Aspe
Fiorello Perez
Foster Friess
Fran Fortier
Frances Fiore
Francesca Azzano
Francisco Fernandez G.
Francisco Zamora
Francisco Zorrilla
Frank & Kathie Lee Gifford
Frank Hannah
Gabriel Reyes
Gary Bauer
George Murray

George Shea
Gerardo Morales
Gilbert Davila
Gissel Gomez
Glenda
Glenn Williams
Gloria Calzada
Gloria Rodriguez
Gov Perry
Governor Rick & Anita Perry
Greg Dunn
Hank Evers
Harry Jackson
Henry Munoz
Howard Ahmanson, Jr.
Ignacio Ortiz
In Memory of Yesenia Orozco
Ivette A. Díaz
J. Peter Sartain
J. Skylar Testa
Jacque Severino
Jaeson Ma
James Dobson
James Murray
Janet Tremblay
Jasmine O'Donnell
Jason & Crystalina Evert
Jason Pastore
Javier Velarde
Jean Lim
Jeb & Columba Bush
Jeff & Marty Flocken
Jeff Freeman
Jeff Hunt
Jeff Smith
Jennifer A. Ruggiero
Jennifer A. Rutledge
Jennifer Nelson
Jenny Korn
Jerry Falwell, RIP
Jim & Angelique Bell
Jim & Elizabeth Graham
Jim Bonshock & Family
Jim Butler
Jim Daly
Jim Hughes
Jim Nolan
Jim Scroggin
Jim Tolle
Joanne Welter
Joe Bonilla
Joe Gigante
Joe O'Farrell

John & Selene Devaney
John Jakubczyk
John Logigian
John Norris
John Sheppard
John Tidwell
Johnny Bolton
Jon Foreman
Jon Secada
Jonathan Baruch
Jonathan Bock
Jonathan Jones
Jorge Berlanga
Joseph F. Naumann
Joseph Hoejs
Josh Taber
Joshua Corby Pons
Juan Chicalana Dominguez Adame
Juan David de Jesus
Juan José Origel
Judy Brown
Julia Osiripaibul
Julie Butler
Kacie Wills
Kara Klein
Karen Carlisle
Karen Colbert
Karen Garnett
Karen Walker
Karol Meynard
Kathie Lee & Frank Gifford
Kathleen Miller
Kathleen Shanahan
Kathy Owen
Kathy Schmugte
Katie McCarthy
Katie Porter
Keet Lewis
Kelli McClendon
Ken Windebank
Kent Peters
Kent Roshau
Keri Brehm
Kevin Gessay
Kim Dorr
Kim Huntsman
Kristan Hawkins
Kristin Hansen
La Familia Baena
La Familia Gomez-Monteverde
La Familia Severino
La Familia Verástegui
Lane Garrison

Lapacazo Sandoval
Laura Thomas
Lauren Hanna
Lee John Bruno
Lee Roy Mitchell
Leith Anderson
Len Muscelli
Lena-Isabella Medina
Lenny Medina
Leonard Leo
Leticia Mendoza
Linda Lucke
Lisa Dallos
Lisa Morton
Lisa Sampson
Liz Disco
Liz Saroki
Lou Engel
Lou Sheldon
Luis Balaguer
Luis Calzada
Luis Cortes
Luis Palau
Maggie DeWitte
Manolo Diaz
Marc Ayers
Marcos Witt
Margarita Cisneros
Margo & Dan Lange
Maria Celeste
Marian Desrosiers
Marianne Luthin
Marie Smith
Marjorie Dannenfelser
Mark Andre
Mark Andreas
Mark Brumley
Mark Foxwell
Mark Frei
Mark Gietzen
Mark Hart
Mark Huddy
Mark Rodgers
Mark Salisbury
Marshall Bush
Marti Gillian
Mary Angelini
Mary Ann Dunn
Mary Boyert
Mary Pat Jahner
Mary T. Shriver
Mathew Staver
Matt Branon

Matt Maes
Matt Maher
Matt Smith
Matthew & Nadine Marsden
Matthew Kelly
Matthew Taylor
Meg Warren
Megan Vargo
Melanie Pritchard-Welsh
Melinda Knight
Melissa Augspurger
Melissa Balaguer
Melissa Charbonneau
Michael Burns
Michael Flaherty
Michael Joseph
Michelle Morales
Michelle Morin
Michelle Santin
Mick Fern
Mickey O'Hare & family
Miguel & Elizabeth Orozco
Miguel Camarago
Mike Alexander
Mike Sweeney
Miki Hill & family
Missy Smith
Mitch Hesley
Monita Alvarez
Monsignor Raymond H. Beard, RIP
Morgan Kondash
Mortan Blackwell
Mouli & Stacy Cohen
Mr. and Mrs. Anthony Hayden
Mr. and Mrs. Christopher
    Wolfington
Mr. and Mrs. Dan Polett
Mr. and Mrs. Eustace W. Mita
Mr. and Mrs. Greg Wierda
Mr. and Mrs. J. Brian O'Neill
Mr. and Mrs. James Delaney
Mr. and Mrs. James J. Maguire
Mr. and Mrs. Matt Gillin
Mr. and Mrs. Michael Barton
Mr. and Mrs. Michael O'Neill
Mr. and Mrs. Thomas McCrory
Mr. and Mrs. Vince O'Neill
Mr. Greg Stefano
Mr. Salisbury
Mrs. Claire Boyle
Neil Cavuto
Neil DeGraide
Nellie Gray

Nicandro Diaz
Nicole LeBlanc
Noreen Johnson
Oswaldo Lainez
Pablo Jose Barroso
Pablo Montero
Pam Wilkie Wright
Pastor Jeff Freeman
Pastor Jim Tolle
Pat & Dan Starkey
Pat McCarthy
Patricio Slim
Patrick Novecosky
Patrick O'Neil
Patti Armond
Patty Marx
Paul Forat
Paul Huber
Paul Pennington
Paul Simoneau
Paul Tripodi
Paul Weyrich
Peg Kenny
Peggy Noonan
Pepe Portillo
Peter Brown
Peter Redpath
Phil Burress
Phil Waugh
Phillip Jauregui
Pilar O'Leary
Pilar Sada Caballero
Piolin
Pope Benedict XVI
Pope John Paul II
Rafael Vazquez
Rafaela Trevino
Rai Rojas
Ramon Cordova
Randy Raus
Raquel Lopez
Raquel Perera
Rayanne Bennett
Raymond Arroyo
Raymond Burke
Raymond Castellon
Raymond Flynn
Respect Life Coordinators
Ricardo Peltier
Richard & Yvonne Seeman
Richard Bernier
Richard Bott
Richard Donley Fox

Richard Land
Richard Perez-Feria
Richard Viguerie
Rick Scarborough
Rob & Berni Neal
Robert Christianson
Roberto Hernandez
Roberto Palazuelos
Rod D. Martin
Rod Parsley
Roger & Carrie Severino
Ron & Cheri Coughlin
Ron Luce
Ron Mitchell
Rory Hoipkemier
Rosalind Moss
Roxana Cobo
Ruben Quezada
Russell Johnson
Ryan Seacrest
Ryan Wolfington
S. Eduardito
S. Filumena
Sally Atwell
Sally Follett
Sally Oberski
Salvatore R. Matano
Sam Brownback
Sarah B. Smith
Scott & Kimberly Hahn
Scott Levy
Sen. Martinez & John Stemberg
Sharon Abruzzo
Sharon Swart
Shawn Crawford
Sister Ave Maria
Social Justice Coordinators
Sorena Perry
Sr. Catherine Marie & S.M.M.E.
St. Michael's Abbey
Stacy Long
Stephanie Becker
Steve & Teresa LeMire
Steve Baldwin
Steve Bartz
Steve Jalsevac
Steve McEveety
Stuart & Nancy Epperson
Stuart Epperson
Sue Melefsky
Suhail Rizvi
Susan B. Anthony
Susan Carroll

Susan Smith
Susanna Herro
Susie Araujo
Suzanne Abdalla
Suzette Chaires
Suzie Spence
T. Allen Humbrecht
Tania Orduña
Tara Maleckovic
Tarek Saab
Ted Baehr
Ted Hurley
Ted Royer
Teresa Tomeo
Teresa Vermeulen
Terrance & Barbara Caster
Terry & Kathy McGaughn
Terry Barber
The Wolfington Family
Thomas Olmsted
Tiffany Lamphere
Tim & Valerie Staples
Tim Busch
Tim Echols
Timothy Drake
Tio Paco
Todd Burns
Tom Allen
Tom Atwood
Tom Campbell
Tomas Cordoba
Tony & Susan Bennett
Tony Perkins
Tony Ryan
Tracey Casale
Tracy Reynolds
Trey Bowles
Tyler Ament
Ulysses Alvarado
V. Guadalupe
Vance Van Patten
Victoria Orbananos
Villareal Family
Virginia Marsh
Walter Yoshimitsu
Wendy Grant
William J. Blacquiere
William Owens
Willow Sanders
Youth and Young Adult
    Coordinators
Yvonne Jimenez
Zip Rzeppa

INTERNS: Full-time

Alejandra Canseco
Alexa Besore
Amy Lechtenberg
Amy Moroney
Ana Garcia
Andrea Lynch
Andrea Miramontes
Anna Paula Dahuss
Anthony Whistler
Auravelia Colomer
Beth Yanez
Brian Salisbury
Christina Brown
Collin Collin
Cynthia Aby
Eddie Gil
Elizabeth Guilford
Erin Hanson
Francisco Rodriguez
Gina Meyers
Isabel Vidal
Jessie Tapel
Joanna Styczenski
Joe Torres
Karina Mennell
Karla Espinosa
Kathleen Bacon
Kevin Kewely
Laura Gonzalez
Lauren Hannah
Leah Smigel
Liz Saroki
Mane Camelo
Mariana Veraza
Mary Bridgwood
Mary Schleich
MaryAnne Garner
Matthew Campbell
Matthew Salisbury
Natalia Fletcher
Natalie Cordray
Sally Gonzalez
Santiago Requejo
Shannon Littleton
Star Tucker
Tash Mallory

INTERNS: Part-time

Erin Braun
Ezequiel Gutierrez
Jeanette Garcia-Montes
Karina Duran
Melissa Jagel
Natalie Moon
Paulina Pina Garcia
Rose Arzate
Salvatore Di Salvator
Wilbanice Ayala

ORGANIZATIONS

American Center for Law and Justice
American Christian School Association
American Family Association
American Heritage Girls
American Life League
American Values
Bethany Christian Services
BNC
Breakpoint
Campaign Life Coalitions
Care Net
Carmelite Sisters
Catholic Answers
Catholic Charities USA
Catholic Kids Net,
Center for Bioethics and Human Dignity
CFRs
Challenge
Christopher West Foundation
CIMA
Clear Staff
Concerned Women for America
Congressional Coalition Adoption Institute
Congressional Hispanic Caucus Institute
ConQuest
Council on Christian Colleges and Universities
Council on Faith in Action (CONFIA)
Daughters of Saint Paul
Dave Thompson Foundation

Esperanza
EWTN
Faith in Action
Family Life
Family Research Council
First Alliance Church
Focus on the Family
Guys For Life
Heartbeat International
Hispanic Leadership Institute
Hombre Nuevo
Human Life International
Justice at the Gates
Knights of Columbus
LARAZA
Latin World Entertainment
Legatus
Legionaries of Christ
LifeTeen
LULAC
Mapat
Matthew Kelly Foundation
Mexican Embassy
Mission Network- Familia,
National Adoption Association
National Association of Evangelicals
National Council for Adoption
National Day of Prayer
National Endowment for the Humanities
National Right to Life
NCA
NCLR
Newman centers
OK Magazine
Opus Dei
Pastor Maldonado Ministries
Project 1.27
Promise Keepers
Pure Fashion
Rachel House
Regnum Christi
Saint Vincent de Paul
Salem Communications
Salvation Army
Shaohannahs Hope
Southern Baptist Convention

St. Agnes Catholic Church and Chapel
Stand True
Students for Life
Susan B. Anthony List
Teen Mania
Teen Pact
Televisa
The Call
The Campaign for Working Families
The Catholic Church
The Center for Bioethics and Human Dignity
The Dove Foundation
The Justice Foundation
The Majella Project
The Mike & Shara Sweeney Family Foundation
The offices of Communication and Public Relations
The offices of Hispanic Activities
The offices of Respect Life
The offices of Social Justice
The offices of Youth and Young Adult Activities
Traditional Values Coalition
Univision
USCCB
Walden Media
Wall Builders
Willow Creek Association
Woods Chapel United Methodist Adoption Foundation
World America Adoption
World Vision
Young Life